The Home School Detectives

# THE MYSTERY OF THE
# CAMPUS CROOK

## John Bibee

**InterVarsity Press**
Downers Grove, Illinois

InterVarsity Press® is the book-publishing division of InterVarsity Christian
Fellowship®, a student movement active on campus at hundreds of universities,
colleges and schools of nursing in the United States of America, and a member
movement of the International Fellowship of Evangelical Students. For information
about local and regional activities, write Public Relations Dept., InterVarsity
Christian Fellowship, 6400 Schroeder Rd., P.O. Box 7895, Madison, WI 53707-7895.

Cover illustration: David Darrow

ISBN 0-8308-1914-2

Printed in the United States of America

**Library of Congress Cataloging in Publication Data**

Bibee, John.
    The mystery of the campus crook/John Bibee.
        p.    cm.  — (The Home School Detectives)
    Summary: When the Home School Detectives respond to the blond
girl's request to help find her missing computer, they become
involved in mysterious deceptions.
    ISBN 0-8308-1914-2 (paper: alk. paper)
    [1. Stealing—Fiction.   2. Christian life—Fiction.   3. Mystery
and detective stories.]   I. Title.   II. Series: Bibee, John.   Home
School Detectives.
PZ7.B471464Mw     1996
[Fic]—dc20                                 96-71
                                              CIP
                                              AC

| 16 | 15 | 14 | 13 | 12 | 11 | 10 | 9 | 8 | 7 | 6 | 5 | 4 | 3 | 2 | 1 |
|----|----|----|----|----|----|----|----|----|----|----|----|----|----|----|----|
| 09 | 08 | 07 | 06 | 05 | 04 | 03 | 02 | 01 | 00 | 99 | 98 | 97 | 96 | | |

# Chapter One

## The Strange Girl

"Emily! Come on!"

"Just a minute." Emily clicked rapidly on the computer keys.

"Now!"

"I'm almost done!" she yelled.

"Mom is ready to go!" Josh Morgan frowned as he entered her room.

"In a minute!" she yelled, not even aware that he had come into her room.

"Lost in cyberspace again?" Josh asked with disgust. "I should have known. Get off that computer and come down to the car. We've got to get to campus."

"The concert isn't for quite a while," Emily said.

"But Mom wants to drop us off at the school, and she needs to leave now or she's going to be late for her meeting."

"Just a minute more." Emily glared at the keyboard as if puzzled.

Josh walked up behind her. He looked at the screen. " 'What's up, Daddy-o?' " Josh read out loud. "Who are you writing to?"

"To Daddy, of course."

"Why did you repeat it so many times? Can't he read?"

"That's the odd part," Emily said. "He's logged on, and I've been trying to do the chat command. That's my sign that I want to talk. Only he's not responding. I wonder if the line is messed up somehow."

"Why do you say 'Daddy-o'?"

"It's just our code. Remember that costume party we had at church last year when everyone dressed like they did in the fifties? They played old records and stuff."

"Yeah," Josh said. "That was a lot of fun."

"Remember how Dad went as a beatnik?"

"That's right. He wore all those black clothes and a beret."

"He was calling everyone 'Daddy-o' that night," Emily said. "He said that's a slang term people used back then. I just liked it because it said 'Daddy.' So on the computer I started calling him Daddy-o. Only today he's not responding for some reason."

"He's probably busy," Josh said impatiently. "Daddy-o must not have time to chat-o and neither do you or else we'll be mucho late-o for Mom's meeting-o. Can you dig that?"

"Okay, okay." Emily began typing rapidly.

" 'We . . . are . . . going . . . to . . . the . . . museum . . . now . . . ' " Josh read out loud as Emily typed. " 'If . . . your . . . friends . . . are . . . curious, . . . we . . . are . . . the . . . ones . . . with . . . the . . . instruments . . . playing . . . music . . .' Very funny. He already knows that."

"Don't you have a sense of humor?" Emily kept typing.

"Just hang up," Josh replied. "I don't have a sense of humor when you're making us late."

"It's not good netiquette to just hang up," Emily said. "You're supposed to log out. That way—"

"Just do it!" Josh pointed to his watch. "It's also not good manners to make other people wait on you because you're lost in cyberspace."

"I'm all ready." Emily reached over to flip off her computer with a defiant flare. The screen went dark as she jumped to her feet. She grabbed her flute case. "But you should have seen where I went today on the World Wide Web."

"Come on, come on." Josh guided his sister out the door. He didn't share her enthusiasm for the Internet and all the places you could visit electronically. To him it was sort of interesting, but mostly just a big waste of time.

"I went to the NASA home page and saw the neatest pictures of the solar system. You wouldn't believe how beautiful they look, Josh. They have that new telescope sending back photos all the time. They have dozens of photos. I downloaded some of them so you can see them too. Then I linked over to this Natural History Museum page in—"

"We're late, Emily." Josh led her through the kitchen. "I hope you kept up with your practice on the Mozart piece. You know and I know how much time you've been spending fooling around in cyberspace."

"It's not fooling around!"

"It is when you're supposed to be practicing your music lessons," Josh said. They were almost to the front door.

Emily whirled around and faced her brother. "What are you implying?"

"I'm saying I know how you've been playing a tape recording of your flute lessons so Mom will think you're really practicing when you're not," Josh said.

"How dare you accuse me of . . . of . . ." As Emily's voice got louder her face got redder.

"Of faking it?" Josh frowned. "I don't accuse. I know. I caught you. I was going to log on the computer yesterday at four o'clock from my room, but the line was busy because you were already on. I went to your room to ask you to get off. That's when I heard the music playing."

"You spied on me!" Emily shouted.

"I sure did. I was curious about how you could be playing flute and typing at the computer at the same time. Of course maybe you have two extra arms that you keep hidden from the rest of us. I listened at the door just to make sure. You should have turned up the music a little louder so we couldn't hear the clicking of your computer keyboard. Of course, if the music was too loud, then everyone in the whole house would know it's a recording and not really you playing, wouldn't they?"

Her big brother smiled smugly. Emily's eyes narrowed, but she couldn't think of anything to say. She had been sure no one had noticed what she had been doing. To her it seemed like the perfect way to get a little more time on the computer. After all, visiting places on the World Wide Web was educational, and it wasn't nearly as boring as playing the same piece of music over and over again.

"You . . . you . . . big snoop!" she sputtered.

"I'm just one of the Home School Detectives on the job.

Only this time," Josh opened the front door, "it was at home."

"How dare you spy on me!" Emily stomped her foot. It was true that she and Josh and their friends, Julie and Carlos Brown and Rebecca and Billy Renner, were known around the town of Springdale as the Home School Detectives. Ever since they had solved a thirty-year-old bank robbery case, the name had stuck for their group. She was proud of the crimes they had helped to solve, but she never dreamed her brother would be acting like a detective around her. "That's not being a detective; that's just being a big sneak!"

"Is it?" Josh asked with a smile. "Since I discovered you were faking that time, I've been curious about how many other times you've pretended to practice and been playing on the computer instead. Of course, you know that Mr. Walden has been sick, and we haven't been able to have our regular practices as a group. If the cat is away, the mouse will play . . . on the computer and not on her flute."

"You better watch who you're calling names," Emily said, "or I'll tell Mom."

"I think we *should* tell Mom and Dad." Josh grinned. "I think they would want to hear all about that, don't you think?"

"You wouldn't dare!" Emily followed her brother outside. Suddenly she felt scared. Her brother could ruin everything. She ran to catch up to him as he got into the van. Mrs. Morgan sat in the driver's seat. The engine was running.

"I have a meeting, Emily," Mrs. Morgan said. Emily knew from her tone of voice that her mother wasn't all the way mad, but she was clearly irritated.

"I know that." Emily was trying to be polite even though she was scared. She glared at her brother as she got into the van. She sat in the very back seat. Josh sat in the front passenger seat by his mother. He turned and smiled at her. The van was unusually quiet because their younger brothers, David and Daniel, and their sister, Elizabeth, were all at the Johnsons' house.

Emily was quiet as they rode to the university, where her father taught engineering. Her mother planned to drop her and Josh off early at the museum for their performance. Both parents were then going to a special home school meeting that afternoon and evening in a nearby town. That meant they would miss Emily and Josh's performance. Emily was secretly glad.

Josh talked happily with his mother about a new guitar he was saving up money to buy. Every once in a while he would look back at Emily and smile. His smile made her so mad. She wanted to reach up and slug him, but she knew she would get into trouble. Plus her parents always made her brothers or sister tell why they were upset if they got in fights so the air could be cleared. In this case, Emily preferred that the air not be so clear, so she tried not to show how angry she felt. There was no choice. She was trapped, her brother knew it, and he was enjoying it.

As the van got closer and closer to the university, Emily began to wish she had practiced more. Without the normal series of practices Mr. Walden usually demanded, she had let things slide. She knew most of the pieces they would be playing fairly well. They had played the Mozart piece over a year ago, and she had done okay then. In fact, that was how she was able to make a recording of it. She played it perfectly for the tape, so she figured she didn't need to practice that piece as much. Besides, she just didn't like that piece anyway.

"I'll blend in with the others, and we'll sound good like we always do," Emily tried to convince herself. "I practiced plenty." But the more she told herself that, the more uneasy she felt.

Mrs. Morgan pulled the van into the parking lot of the university museum. There were lots of cars, and the parking lot was full. Several big yellow school buses were parked in spaces reserved just for buses.

"The new exhibit has been very popular in other cities," Mrs. Morgan said. "Since this is the first day, there are more people than normal. I hope you have a good crowd at the reception when you children play."

Josh and Emily were part of a musical group made up of home schooled friends. Emily played the flute, Josh played the guitar and bass, Julie played the violin, Carlos played the keyboard, Rebecca played the cello, and Billy played the drums. Billy wasn't playing that afternoon because they didn't need drums for the pieces they planned to play.

Mr. Walden, a retired professor and music teacher, was the conductor. The group had never had a formal name, though Mr. Walden sometimes called them Walden's Musical Wonders when he was in a very good mood. He was a nice man and a member of their church, but he was a very strict teacher. Sometimes he was just too fussy about things, Emily thought. She had complained about Mr. Walden's practice demands to her parents many times. She had been secretly glad when several of the practices had to be canceled because of his recent illness.

"He's interested in bringing out the best in you children," Emily's father had said one night at the supper table. "He's demanding, but that's good. He never demands that you perform something you're incapable of performing."

"This performance at the museum reception is impossible," Emily had replied. "The music is too hard."

"No, it's not," Josh had added. "It's a stretch, especially that piece by Mozart, but we can do it if we practice. We've played it before and we did okay."

"It's too many notes too fast," Emily had replied glumly.

"Mr. Walden is always very proud of the way you play," her mom had said. "I'm sure you all can do it if he thinks you can. He knows your abilities well enough by now. It's too bad that his sickness has caused you to miss your normal rehearsal schedule."

"We should just cancel the concert," Emily had said.

"Mr. Walden thinks you can handle it, even if he has been sick," Mrs. Morgan had said. "And the museum committee did not want you to cancel. They're really counting on you. When you start to play, I'm sure you'll sail right through all the pieces and make beautiful music."

In the parking lot, Emily looked down with dismay at her folder of music. The day of the concert had arrived, but she didn't feel like she was going to sail through anything. When she really knew a piece of music well, there was a very familiar feeling to all the fingerings, as if they became automatic after a while, so she could play it almost without looking at the music. Mr. Walden said they should get so familiar with their music that they could play it in their sleep. He was joking, of course, but what he meant was that he expected them to know their music extremely well before they performed. But Emily didn't have that confident feeling about the Mozart piece.

Josh opened the van's rear door and got out his electric bass and electric guitar. Emily carried her flute, the music stands and the music folders. She said good-bye to her mom, who was going to wait for Josh to unload the rest of his equipment and then pick up their dad for the home school meeting.

"I hope a lot of people don't show up," Emily said glumly as she looked around at the very full parking lot. "We should have canceled this performance."

"Why is that, Emily?" Josh said a little bit too sweetly. "I didn't think you got nervous when we performed."

"Just be quiet, Josh," Emily said. "I don't even want to talk to you."

Emily started walking across the parking lot when she noticed a young woman with very short, bright yellow-blond hair sitting on a stone wall by the museum steps. Because of her odd appearance, she was hard not to notice. She looked old enough to be a university student, though she could have been in high school. She was dressed in old black jeans, a dark T-shirt, and black-and-white high-top canvas tennis shoes.

What caught Emily's attention besides the unusual shade of blond hair, which was obviously bleached, were the big silver earrings. Emily had pierced ears, but not like this girl. Each ear was pierced in several places, not only in the earlobe, but also halfway up the side. She had never seen so many earrings in one ear. Emily tried not to stare, but it was hard because the girl was looking back at her. For a moment, it seemed like the girl was going to say something to her. Emily looked down at her feet, embarrassed that she'd been caught staring.

Emily followed her older brother into the front entrance to the museum. As Emily got to the big doors, she looked back. The blond girl with all the earrings was coming up the steps behind her. She looked right into Emily's eyes. Emily looked away, feeling embarrassed again.

Emily walked quickly through the big open doors of the museum. The reception was going to be downstairs. She knew the way since their group had played there six months earlier when the museum was hosting an exhibition of impressionist paintings.

The current exhibit was called *The Printed Word*. The museum walls were covered with examples of printing from hundreds of years ago. The frames and cases were filled with old playing cards, posters and pamphlets with historical significance. The most famous and valuable part of the exhibit was a copy of the Gutenberg Bible, the first book printed with movable type. The two heavy volumes were kept inside a big protective case right in the middle of the room.

The museum was crowded with people. Lines of elementary school students stamped their feet impatiently as they waited to take the guided tour of the exhibit. People were everywhere, moving this way and that. Voices echoed in the big room.

Emily followed Josh to a side hall with an elevator. Josh pushed a button. As they waited for the elevator, Emily looked back into the big exhibition room. The blond girl from outside was walking straight toward Emily from across the far side of the room. Emily began to feel a bit uneasy. The elevator doors opened. Emily hurried inside. Josh followed her. Emily turned around. The big elevator doors were sliding shut when she saw the blond girl still walking toward them. She seemed to be looking straight at Emily.

"Wow!" Emily was relieved as the doors shut. "Did you see that girl coming toward the elevator? I think she was following me."

"What girl?" Josh was looking down at his guitar case. One

of the latches had flipped open, and he was trying to shut it by pressing it against his leg.

"The blond girl with all the earrings. She was right outside when we came into the museum, and it looks like she's following me," Emily said. "You didn't see her? She has about a dozen earrings in each ear. She looks really strange."

"Why would someone be following you?" Josh asked.

"I don't know."

"You're just imagining things."

"I guess so." For the first time that day Emily was glad to be with Josh.

The elevator doors whooshed open on the lowest level. The children walked out and down the hall until they came to a set of double doors. Josh pushed, and the door opened into a large room. A man was setting up tables for a meal. Up front there was a lectern. Off to the right was a small stage where they were going to play.

"I guess none of the others are here yet." Josh walked over to the small stage. Five metal chairs were sitting on the stage. He set down his bass and guitar cases. Emily put her things down too. Josh looked out over the tables from the stage. "There will be lots of people here."

"Yeah," Emily said without enthusiasm. "Why didn't we just cancel? Mr. Walden has been too sick. I wish Dad had never volunteered us for this job."

"Relax, you'll probably do okay," Josh said. "At least I hope you do. I'm going back outside for the amplifiers. Mom's still waiting."

"Okay," Emily said. Josh trotted out of the room. Emily frowned as she looked at all the tables. She sat down on a little metal chair on the stage. She opened her music folder and began looking at the pieces.

"Why didn't I practice more?" she moaned softly to herself as she looked at the Mozart piece. There was one place in particular where she would practically be playing a solo. The flute and cello were the only instruments playing for several bars. Emily sighed and began to feel another wave of panic. "Look at all those notes."

She was so busy staring at the music that she didn't notice the girl with blond hair and lots of earrings enter the room. In fact, Emily didn't notice the girl as she walked past the tables and up to the little stage. Emily reached down to pick up her flute case. That's when she saw the girl's black pants and tennis shoes. Emily jerked her head up.

The girl looked straight into Emily's eyes. Emily reared back. She stood up, looking out over the big room. No one else was in sight. The man setting the tables was gone. Josh was gone. For a moment the girl just stared at Emily very intensely.

"Are you Emily Morgan?" the girl finally asked.

"Yes."

"Professor Morgan's daughter?"

"That's right." Emily looked around the big room nervously. She had never felt more alone in all her life. A few floors above there were hundreds of people all over the museum, but down here it was just her and this strange person.

"I've got to talk to you." The blond girl's eyes were very intense. "It's a matter of life and death."

# Chapter Two

---

# Astrid

W hat do you want?" Emily glanced anxiously around the big room. Where was Josh? Where were the other people? Emily wished someone, anyone, would show up so she didn't have to be alone with this odd girl.

"I need your help," the girl replied.

"I don't know how I could help you." Emily dropped her music. "We are just here to play for the reception. My brother will be back. The others will be here soon too."

"You'd have time to help me before the concert," the girl said eagerly. "I really would like your help. I can pay you some money."

"Pay me money?" Emily asked in surprise.

"For your services. You are one of those Home School Detectives, aren't you?"

"Well, yeah," Emily said slowly. "How did you know about that?"

"Because I saw stories and pictures in the newspaper, and your father has talked about you in class."

"You're one of my father's students?" Emily asked.

"Yes, and he's mentioned you and Josh and your friends and how you've helped solve crimes. He's bragged about all of you lots of times and put newspaper clippings on his bulletin board."

"I didn't know he talked about us in class too." Emily had finished picking up her music and was now sitting back in her chair.

"He's done it a number of times," the girl said seriously. "He's very proud of you. I wish my dad was that proud of me. I think everyone in my family is embarrassed that I exist."

"Oh." Emily was unsure of what to say.

The girl looked down at her feet, and then looked back up. "Will you help me? Like I said, I can pay—not a lot, but I could pay you a hundred dollars. And I'll pay you more if we're successful. I'm offering a reward."

"A hundred dollars? We don't usually charge for helping people. It's not like we're professional detectives."

"But I would pay you. That's only fair. And I really could use your help."

Over the girl's shoulder, Emily saw Josh pulling a handcart carrying two black-and-gray amplifiers. Emily was never so glad to see Josh in her life.

"My brother is here," Emily said. "We need to set up for the reception."

"Yes, I know," the blond girl said. "That's why I came over here. Your father told me you would be here today."

"Did he say we would help you with detective work?"

"I didn't ask him about that. He just said if we wanted to hear some good classical music to come to the reception. He's proud of your musical abilities too."

"Hi." Josh wheeled the cart over to the little stage. He looked back and forth between Emily and the girl.

"My name is Astrid." The girl extended her hand. "Astrid Flacker."

"I'm Josh Morgan." He shook her hand.

"Astrid wants to hire us as detectives," Emily said slowly. "She's in one of Daddy's classes. He's talked about us in class."

"The Home School Detectives are famous around the campus." Then, for the first time, Emily saw Astrid smile. Even though she looked strange with her yellow-blond hair and earrings, she had a warm smile.

"How do you think we could help you?" Josh asked curiously.

"I had a computer stolen," Astrid said. "A notebook computer. I have to get it back. It has my master's thesis in it, on the hard drive. It's life or death for me, at least for my academic career."

"You didn't make any backups?" Emily asked in surprise.

"I made three backups," Astrid said in anger. "I'm very careful to make backup copies. I'm an electrical engineering major. But all the copies were in my carrying case with the computer. I never thought it would get stolen. I have to get it back. The computer can be replaced, but not all my work. My notes and everything were on the computer."

"That's awful," Emily said sympathetically. "I lost a report I was doing one time. The power went off, and I hadn't saved my work. But that was just a few hours of typing."

"This was work I've been doing for just over a year," Astrid said bitterly. "I was out with a friend having coffee. When I went back to my room, it was gone. It happened five days ago."

"Did you tell the police?"

"Yeah, sure," Astrid said with exasperation. "I told the campus police, and they filed a report with the city police. But they said not to get my hopes up. Something like a computer is hard to find. After I filed my report, they said there was nothing else they could do except notify me if it showed up."

"But you don't think that's going to happen?" Josh asked.

"It doesn't seem likely. But I've *got* to get my stuff back. At least I have to try."

"But how do you think we could help you?" Emily asked.

"Well, I've been asking questions around campus," Astrid said. "Since the campus police didn't seem to be making any progress, I decided to investigate myself."

"Sounds like you're a detective too," Josh said with a smile.

"Not by choice," Astrid said sadly. "It may be a waste of time, but I've got to try to get my computer back. I've offered rewards and put notices up on bulletin boards around campus and even on the electronic bulletin boards that I know the students use."

"A reward?" Emily asked.

"Yeah, I've offered a thousand dollars to someone if they'll give my computer back to me."

"Wow!" Josh said. "That's a lot of money."

"The work on my thesis is worth a lot more than that to me," Astrid said anxiously.

"But how can we help you if the police can't?" Emily asked.

"That's the tricky part," Astrid said. "Like I told you, I've been snooping around. I think I might know who stole my computer."

"Then why don't you just tell the police?" Josh asked. "Couldn't they get it back?"

"Well, I'm not exactly sure who has it," Astrid said with a frown. "You have to be pretty sure for the police to do much."

"So how could we help you?" Josh asked.

"I want to investigate some on my own, but I sort of need some friends or partners to help me investigate," Astrid replied.

"Why wouldn't you just get some of your friends on campus to help you?" Josh asked.

"Because I'm not sure who my real friends are anymore," Astrid said bitterly. "In fact, I think it might have been some of my friends who stole my computer. I don't know who I can trust anymore. That's when I thought of you guys. I know you can be trusted."

"You mean your own friends would steal from you?" Emily asked.

"Maybe," Astrid said.

"Sounds like you could use some new friends," Josh added.

"Yeah, I know that now," Astrid said, her voice cracking with anger. "Won't you please help me? Like I said, I'll pay you just to help. And besides, I'll even give you the reward if we find the computer. A thousand dollars."

"I'd like to help you," Emily said. "And you don't need to pay us anything, does she, Josh?"

"We don't usually work for money," Josh said. "But we do have our concert performance at the reception. That's why we're here."

"We could do it before the concert," Astrid said eagerly. "If we're lucky, I'll just need you for about twenty minutes, tops."

"You mean you don't want us to look for clues?" Emily asked.

"Not at all," Astrid said.

"Then what do you need us for?" Josh asked.

"I have a plan, but I need someone to help me with it," Astrid said. "There's a place just a few blocks from here where I want to look for my computer. Please help me. I really need someone, and I don't know who else to turn to."

"We have time, don't we, Josh? Mom dropped us off early." Emily felt sorry for the girl, especially since it was a computer that had been stolen.

"I guess so." Josh frowned. "I'm still not sure what you want us to do if we're not looking for clues."

"Just come with me, and I'll explain it when we get there," Astrid said. "Please."

"I'd like to help you," Emily said eagerly. "I would hate it if someone stole my computer. What kind of notebook did you have?"

"A Toshiba," Astrid said. "I've had three of them over the years, and they're great. I kept upgrading to new models every few years."

"Did it have a color or mono display?"

"Color, with a gigabyte hard drive, thirty-two megs of RAM," Astrid said, "and a twenty-eight-point-eight modem."

"Wow, that sounds like a powerful machine."

"It was a *great* computer." Astrid looked back and forth between Emily and Josh. "Will you help? Please?"

"Let's go then," Josh said. "But we can't stay too long."

"Great," Astrid said. Josh pushed the handcart behind the little stage and left it. As they walked toward the elevators, two men entered the room. One was an older man with short gray hair and an expensive suit. The other was much younger, very tall and big. The younger man wore a gray uniform-type jacket. A badge on the jacket said *Rod Williams: Museum Guard.*

"I'm going to pull my hair out if that stupid fire alarm goes off one more time," the older man said. "Yesterday was the third false alarm, and the fire department is tired of coming down here every fifteen minutes."

"I don't like it either," the big guard said. "But hey, I'm just a guard. I don't understand those electronic things."

"I know," the older man said with a sigh. When he saw Josh and Emily, his face lit up with a smile.

"Josh and Emily Morgan," the older man said. "It's so good to see you again."

"Hi, Mr. Bunson," Josh said. Mr. Bunson was the assistant director of the museum. Emily recognized him. He looked very small next to the big guard.

"We're looking forward to great music today," Mr. Bunson said. "I was telling Rod earlier about your musical abilities."

"Thanks," Emily said. The big guard smiled easily. He stared at Astrid for a moment, looking especially at her wild blond hair.

"Did you say the fire alarm went off?" Josh asked.

"Yes," Mr. Bunson said. "It's been a nightmare. All false alarms. We don't know if they have been from the thunderstorms or power surges, or what's causing them. But they've been an absolute nuisance. Three false alarms in two days."

Three women walked into the room. They each wore a pretty pastel dress and lots of heavy, sparkling jewelry.

"Hello, Mrs. Bunson," Emily said to the woman in blue.

"Hello, dear," Mrs. Bunson said sweetly. "You make our little fundraising events that much more special. I've told everyone to expect a top-notch performance at the reception."

"We'll do our best," Josh said. The other women looked at Astrid with blank stares. One frowned, looking at all the earrings in her ears.

"We need to run," Emily said.

"All right, children," Mrs. Bunson said. "We'll see you in a little while."

Astrid led the way. They went upstairs in the elevators. As they walked out into the big exhibition hall, the room seemed even more crowded. More students had arrived. The big room echoed with noisy voices.

"Can you wait here?" Astrid asked. "I need to use the restroom."

"We'll wait," Emily said.

"Thanks." Astrid then walked quickly away.

Several university students with bright blue jackets were acting as tour guides for the exhibit. Emily recognized one of the student tour guides, Wendy Phillips, a member of their church in Springdale. She was a beautiful girl with long red hair and a wonderful smile. She was also a school cheerleader. She waved at Emily. Emily smiled and waved back. She was glad that Wendy had noticed her.

"That's Wade Wyoming next to Wendy," Josh said.

"Who's he?"

"Who's he?" Josh repeated in surprise. "He's the star quarterback of the football team. He'll probably get drafted by a pro team. He's been out of action the last few weeks because his arm is hurt. But he should be back soon."

"He sure is big." Emily looked at the tall, handsome student.

"Hey, Wade!" Josh yelled across the room. Wade flashed a smile at Josh and waved back.

"Does he know you?" Emily asked.

"Of course not. But it looks like he knows Wendy."

"Yeah." Emily noticed that Wade and Wendy were leading a tour group together. Lots of young schoolchildren also knew about Wade. Some were asking him for autographs. Josh was tempted to get an autograph himself, especially when it was almost a sure thing that the quarterback would be drafted into the NFL someday.

"Do you think we can really help Astrid get her computer back?" Emily asked.

"I don't know," Josh said with a frown. "She seems odd to me."

"I think she really needs our help," Emily said. "You can't tell everything about someone just by their appearance. She is one of Daddy's students."

"I know. I just have a feeling that there's more to this story than we're getting. I still don't understand what we're supposed to do."

"Here she comes. I guess we'll find out about her plan soon enough."

"I'm ready," Astrid said seriously. "Let's go."

The blond student led the way out through the big hall toward the front doors. They had to wait at the door as another whole busload of students filed inside. After they passed, Astrid motioned for them to go outside.

Outside, the sky was getting cloudier and darker. Astrid frowned at the clouds. "I hope it doesn't rain on us. But it's only a few blocks from here, anyway. Follow me."

Astrid crossed the green grass around the art museum. She walked faster than most people, and Emily almost had to run to keep up. They passed the big natural history and science museum. The young woman led the way across the parking lot to the street. They walked down the sidewalk for a block and then crossed the street.

"It's right over there on the next block," Astrid said.

"What is?"

"That big house," Astrid said. "We're off campus now, but that's a fraternity house."

"What's a fraternity?" Emily asked.

"It's a kind of student social club," Josh said. "They usually have Greek alphabet letters as the names of the clubs. Men are in fraternities and women are in sororities, right?"

"Yes," Astrid said. "Most members of fraternities live in the big fraternity houses instead of the dorms or apartments."

"Are you in a sorority?" Emily asked.

"They don't let people like me in clubs like that," Astrid said. "In fact, that's why I need you two to help me."

"I still don't understand what you want us to do," Josh said as they walked across the street toward the fraternity house.

"Let's go around to the side," Astrid said mysteriously as they got near the big three-story house. Three tall oak trees shaded the front lawn.

"That's a huge house," Emily said as they followed Astrid. The third story had a balcony. A huge trellis with rosebushes leaned against the side of the house.

"What do you want us to do?" Josh asked.

"Inside the front door there's a desk, and there will be a guy behind the desk," Astrid said. "I want you to go inside and give him this envelope. The guy's name is Carl."

The blond girl pulled a plain white envelope out of her back pocket. She gave it to Emily. *Carl* was written on the outside of the envelope.

"What's in it?" Josh asked.

"Just a note." Astrid looked at her watch. "Please do it. But don't tell him I gave you the note."

"Just give him this envelope, and ask him to read it?" Josh asked. "And you don't want us to tell him you gave it to us."

"That's all I need." Astrid's eyes were pleading.

"This is kind of strange detective work," Josh said slowly. "I guess that's the way it happens sometimes."

"I'll give him the note," Emily said.

"Don't tell him it's from me or even mention me, please," Astrid added. "It won't work if they think I'm around."

"Okay," Emily said. Astrid stood behind a big oak tree near a corner of the house.

"This seems pretty weird," Josh muttered as they walked up the steps of the big house.

"I think it's kind of mysterious and exciting," Emily said. "It's like being detectives on television."

"I don't know," Josh said warily.

They opened the big front door of the house and walked inside. Just as Astrid had told them, a student was sitting behind a desk in front of a big set of wooden stairs. A large living room with three couches and some chairs and a big television was off to the right. A hallway led down to the left.

"Are you Carl?" Emily asked.

"Yes," he said with a handsome smile.

"We have this note for you." Emily handed the note across the desk.

"A note?" Carl asked. He took the envelope. He opened it and read it.

"He must be real busy today," Carl said. "Thank you. Tell him I'll check it out. He must have been too busy to call if he sent you two with a note." He looked with a questioning face at Emily.

"I guess," Emily said, shrugging her shoulders.

"I'll take care of it," Carl said with a smile. He stood up and started down the hallway. Emily and Josh stood in front of the desk. Carl looked at them with surprise. "You can tell him I'll check it out, okay? Bye."

Carl turned and walked down the hall. The lobby was empty. "I guess we just go now," Josh said.

"Okay," Emily added. They turned to open the front door. As they walked out, Astrid darted up the steps.

"I'll meet you back at the museum later," Astrid whispered as she rushed past them. She walked quickly around the desk and then started up the stairs. She stopped for a second to look back at the surprised faces of Emily and Josh. She held her finger up to her lips, as if telling them to be quiet, then waved her hand as if to shoo them away. Then she turned and tiptoed up the broad wooden stairs until she was out of sight.

# Chapter Three

---

# The Tour

**W**hat was that all about?" Josh stood with Emily outside and across the street from the big fraternity house. He looked at the upper floor windows, wondering if he would see Astrid.

"I don't know," Emily said. "I guess she thinks her computer is in that house."

"This is really weird." Josh was frowning. "I mean, we just helped someone sneak into a place where she obviously wouldn't be welcome under normal circumstances."

"We didn't know she would sneak in."

"I wonder if we should tell Carl."

"But that would spoil Astrid's plan," Emily said.

"But what's her plan?" Josh asked. "We don't know what she's doing in there."

"But what if Astrid is right? What if her computer is in there and she's just getting it back?"

"But what if all that was a big lie and she's up to no good? Maybe we should call the police."

"But we agreed to help her. She trusted us. We can't say we'll help her and then call the police on her. That's like breaking our word."

"I never promised to help her sneak into someone's house. We were tricked into helping her do that, and I don't like to be tricked." Josh looked at his watch.

"But she could be telling us the truth," Emily said. "Maybe her stolen computer is in there."

"I think we need to wait here and see what she does," Josh said firmly. "We can sit behind that bush over there and see what happens. But if she comes out with anything besides a notebook computer, I think we should call the police or tell Carl or do something."

"I guess that's fair enough." Emily hated to think that Astrid had lied to them.

The two detectives hid behind some evergreens near the curb. Emily stared at the upstairs windows, wondering if she would see Astrid. Josh sighed. He didn't feel like waiting around, yet he felt obligated.

"We should pray about all this because we sure need wisdom," Josh said after they had waited for almost five minutes.

"That's probably a good idea," Emily said. "We should have thought of it before. I wonder how she planned to get out without being seen?"

"I don't think she had a plan. Look." Josh pointed.

The front door of the big house flew open. Carl and three other fraternity students surrounded Astrid as they shoved her out the door.

"You come snooping around here again and we'll call the

cops!" one of the guys yelled.

"Troublemaking weirdo!" another guy shouted.

"I didn't do anything!" Astrid yelled. The guys kept pushing, and Astrid almost fell down the steps. She staggered and
swayed but managed to keep on her feet. The guys stood
together in the doorway, blocking it and shouting as Astrid
walked down the sidewalk.

"What should we do?" Emily asked.

"Let's just watch and see where she goes," Josh said. "We
did what she asked. I think we ought to stay out of this
business. We don't know enough to get involved."

"You may be right. But what if Astrid is telling the truth?
I would want someone to help me get my computer back if it
was stolen."

"We tried to help her, and it didn't work." Josh felt confused. "Let's go back to campus. It looks like Astrid is going
that way."

Emily and Josh watched the blond girl carefully. She
walked quickly without looking back.

"She really moves along," Josh said. Astrid began to jog
when she hit the campus. She disappeared between the two
museums.

"Let's go," Josh said. He and Emily followed her. When
they rounded the corner of the museum, the girl with blond
hair was nowhere in sight.

"Where do you think she went?" Emily asked.

"She might have gone into the museum. We need to go
back ourselves. We're supposed to take the tour of the exhibit
before we perform."

Josh and Emily walked back to the front of the museum.
As they went inside, Emily quickly surveyed the big room,

looking for Astrid's bright yellow hair. Josh was looking too.

"Let's check downstairs," Josh said. Emily nodded. The brother and sister headed for the elevator.

The reception room downstairs was filling up, but there was no sign of Astrid. Many people were already seated and were drinking and talking. The plates of food would be brought out soon, and whatever it was smelled very good to Emily.

Rebecca Renner was standing in front of the stage. Julie and Carlos Brown were arranging their music and instruments. Off to the side, Mr. Walden was talking to Mrs. Bunson. Emily suddenly felt a twinge of guilt when she saw Mr. Walden. In the excitement of trying to help Astrid, she had forgotten about the concert.

"Here are the rest of my musicians now," Mr. Walden said, beaming.

"Hi, Mr. Walden," Josh said. "I hope you're feeling better."

"I'm much better, thank you," he said.

"Hello, Mr. Walden," Emily mumbled.

"Are you sick, Emily?" Mr. Walden asked with a look of concern.

"No, sir," Emily said. She then wished she had said she was sick, like Mr. Walden had been. That would have given her an acceptable excuse if she played badly. But Emily was seldom sick. She knew no one would believe an excuse like that. She had not been to a hospital a day in her life, not even when she was born. She had been born at home, and her mother had used midwives to help deliver her. Josh had been born at a hospital, but the rest of the children had been born at home.

"We should have a very good turnout," Mr. Walden said

cheerfully. "Mrs. Bunson thinks there will be more people today than for the event we played for the last time."

"That's great," Josh said. "I hope they can raise lots of money for the museum."

"I hope they pass the hat *before* we play," Emily muttered to herself.

"The other home schoolers are waiting upstairs," Billy Renner said as he ran over to the group. Billy, Rebecca's twin brother, had been keeping watch upstairs. "We're supposed to go on our tour now."

The others were part of the Springdale home school co-op, a loose organization of home school families in and around Springdale. The families that home schooled got together for special events on a regular basis, like field trips to the museum. The co-op had a monthly newsletter they sent through the regular mail. For those with computers, which were almost all the families, they also had an electronic mailing list.

But the most popular computing addition was the World Wide Web page the co-op had set up. The WWW page, or home page, as it was called, was like the co-op's own private electronic information page. It was linked to other home schooling home pages in other parts of the country. Besides that, there were links to lots of Web pages of educational interest, like NASA and the Library of Congress. Every day there were new and exciting home pages that were being added, and you could link up with only a click of a button. Exploring all those links was hard to resist for curious computer people like Emily. She knew that you could always find more and more links and more places to visit with new sights to see. It was like traveling around the world without even leaving your desk chair.

"Children, you are wanted upstairs for your tour of the exhibit, *The Printed Word*," Mrs. Bunson announced.

All the children except Emily rushed toward the elevators. She dragged her feet all the way.

"Come on, Emily!" Billy yelled at her from inside the elevator.

"I'm coming," Emily grumbled as she sped up a little.

"What's the matter with her?" Billy asked Josh.

"Maybe she's nervous about performing," Josh said with a dry grin.

"Be quiet, Josh!" Emily spat out. "I *will* get nervous if you keep bugging me." The other kids in the elevator looked at Emily in surprise. She and Josh usually got along pretty well, and they were surprised at her outburst.

The main room of the museum was still noisy, but a little less crowded. Emily followed Josh and the others across the ceramic tile floor. The other home school co-op children were waiting together in a group at the lobby desk. As Emily crossed the room, she saw bright yellow-blond hair across the room. Astrid was leaning against the wall. She waved at Emily.

Emily wanted to tell Josh, but he was already busy talking to some of his friends in the co-op. Emily stopped and waited. Astrid walked over.

"Thanks for helping me," Astrid said earnestly. "They found me and kicked me out."

"That's too bad," Emily said.

"I got to investigate awhile, but I didn't find what I was looking for," the blond girl quickly added. "There are a couple of other places I need to check out—"

"Emily, let's go," Julie Brown yelled. "Our tour is starting."

Emily turned around. Wendy Phillips and Wade Wyoming were standing near the home school group. Apparently they were going to be the tour guides. Wendy and Wade were both looking at Emily. Wendy waved for Emily to come over. Josh waved for her to come too.

"I've got to go," Emily said, turning back to tell Astrid, but the blond girl had already walked away. Emily was surprised that she hadn't even said good-bye.

"That girl you were talking to is Astrid Flacker, and you ought to stay away from her," Wendy Phillips said as Emily walked over. Wade Wyoming nodded in agreement.

"Do you know her?" the big football star asked.

"Not really," Emily said truthfully. "She's in one of my father's classes."

"Yes, she's an electrical engineering major," Wendy said. "But she's been in a lot of trouble in the past."

"What kind of trouble?" Josh asked.

"Well, she's been in jail before. I do know that," Wendy said softly.

"Jail?" Emily asked in surprise.

"Sure," Wendy said. "She tried to keep it a big secret, but it got out."

"For crimes she committed with computers," Wade Wyoming added. "She's supposed to be some kind of genius when it comes to computer stuff. She's one of those hacker nerds, you know? People around here call her Flacker the Hacker."

"She went to jail?" Emily asked. Her mouth dropped open.

"I could tell you a lot more," Wade said in hushed tones. "But we need to start the tour. I'd stay away from her if I were you. She's nothing but trouble. In fact, I got a call a little while ago. Some of the guys at my frat house found her sneaking around over there. She was probably trying to steal something. They tossed her out on her ear. I told them they should have called the police on the little thief."

"See, I told you there was something fishy about her," Josh said triumphantly as Wade and Wendy walked away. "I just hope that Wade doesn't find out that we helped her get into his fraternity house. I didn't know he lived there."

"Well, I didn't know any of this stuff either," Emily whispered back. "I just met her today. But she's not in jail now. What she said still could be true."

"But she could also be a great big liar," Josh whispered back. "And we helped her sneak into that frat house."

Emily looked around the room. Astrid stood next to the entrance door. She was watching them.

"She's watching us from over by the door," Emily whispered to Josh.

"Let her watch," Josh said. "We need to start the tour."

The group began moving across the room toward a distant wall. Wendy and Wade had given their tour speech so many times that they hardly had to refer to their notes.

"The slow development of movable metal type transformed the world of communications," Wade said as they came to the first piece. "Until the coming of radio a hundred years ago, the printed word was the king of communication the world over."

"That's right," Wendy added with a smile. "Through the printed word, ideas and philosophies spread to the masses of people. As more and more books and materials were printed, more people were able to read and become educated. Many people don't realize it today, but the first printed documents weren't on paper, but were on animal skins called parchments or vellum, like our first example here. Vellum came from the skin of newly born calves or lambs."

"Poor lambs," Julie Brown muttered to Emily. Julie had a very soft heart when it came to animals. Emily tried to pay attention, but she found her mind caught up by other things. Part of the time she wondered about Astrid, and the rest of the time she worried about the upcoming performance. She drifted along with the tour group throughout the museum, barely hearing what Wade and Wendy were saying.

Some of the children asked questions during the tour. Emily looked at the different examples of printing. Most of them were impossible for her to read since they were in German or Latin. Even the examples of printed English were hard to read because the letters looked so strange and the spelling was often different from what she was used to.

In the next big room of the museum, they saw examples of old printing presses and books with illustrations. Those were a little more interesting to her, but she still found it hard to concentrate.

The tour ended up in front of the copy of the big Gutenberg Bible. The home schoolers all crowded around the old Bible for a better look. Emily got closer.

"The Bible has long been considered one of the most valuable books in the world," Wade said. "But until Johann Gutenberg came along, all Bibles had to be copied by hand, a slow, tedious process. But Gutenberg's Bibles, printed from 1450 until 1455, revolutionized the world. About one hundred and eighty copies were originally printed. One hundred and fifty were printed on paper, and thirty on parchment. Only forty-eight copies exist today."

"How much are they worth?" Josh asked.

"No complete Bibles have been sold recently, but they are easily worth millions of dollars," Wade said with a smile. All the children gasped. "Even single pages of the Gutenberg Bible are worth thousands of dollars."

Emily leaned in for a closer look. The two volumes of the Bible under the glass case were both open. Jason Cooper, one of the home schoolers who knew some Latin, was trying to pronounce the words he could read.

"This is the book of Genesis," Jason announced as he read further down the page.

"That's right," Wendy added. "The colorful pictures and lettering around the printed text are called illumination and rubrication. These colorful additions were added by hand by artisans all over Europe. Each Bible also had its own unique binding. The original Bibles were sold to monasteries or to the royal libraries of kings."

"Today anyone can buy a Bible at the corner grocery store for a few dollars, or even be given one for free." Wade held up a copy of a Gideon Bible.

"Ever-changing technologies in the computer field continue to revolutionize the way we learn and communicate." Wendy held up a CD-ROM computer disk. "One disk like this one holds several versions of the Bible, as well as commentaries and dictionaries and a whole library of texts. The world has come a long way since Gutenberg successfully printed his forty-two-line Bible that started the revolution known as the printed word."

The tour was over. The children clapped. Wade and Wendy smiled. Some of the boys rushed in closer to Wade to get his autograph and talk about football. Josh was with the boys, talking to Wade. Emily looked at the old Bible some more.

"I'm glad I don't have to lug that to church and back,"

Rebecca Renner said as she looked at the two heavy volumes. "You'd have to wear two backpacks to carry that around. And it looks like it weighs a ton."

"I know," Emily agreed. She pulled her own small New Testament out of her pocket. She always carried the small book with her. "I'd much rather carry this one."

"I know," Rebecca said. "I'd like having the CD-ROM version myself."

"Yeah, me too," Emily agreed. "If you had that and a notebook with a CD-ROM drive, just think how much—"

A long scream suddenly rose up above all the noise of talking voices. It was so piercing that everyone in the whole museum stopped talking. The scream faded. For a moment there was dead silence.

"What was that?" Emily demanded.

"Where was it?" Rebecca echoed.

"Upstairs!" someone shouted.

"Downstairs!" another voice cried out.

"By the elevators!" other voices shouted out. Emily turned and looked. A crowd was developing in front of the elevators. Emily pushed her way through the crowd. Two men were squatting by someone lying on the floor by the stairwell. All Emily could see were black-and-white high-top tennis shoes and black jeans.

"That looks like . . . " Emily started to say, when one of the men moved. A flash of bright yellow hair came into view.

Astrid was slumped back against the wall near the stairs. Her eyes were shut and her head was flopped to one side. A trickle of blood ran from her nose.

"Someone call a doctor!" one of the men shouted as he looked up at the crowd. "Call a doctor now!"

# Chapter Four

## The Alarm

**T**he crowd around the fallen girl grew larger. Emily moved to the side of the hallway and flattened herself against the far wall. She didn't want to miss what happened.

"Her name is Astrid Flacker," Emily said to one of the men.

"She's unconscious," a man with white hair said.

The noise of the growing crowd was getting louder. People were peering at the girl, asking questions.

"I think Dr. Renner might be downstairs," Emily said, but nobody paid attention. Dr. Renner was Billy and Rebecca's father. She opened the stairwell door. She bounded down the steps, hanging on to the rail loosely with one hand as she sped as fast as she could go. By the time she reached the reception hall she was breathing fast.

Most people were seated at the tables, and the food was being served. The room smelled delicious. Emily scanned the tables. She wasn't sure whether Dr. Renner was coming to the reception or not, but she thought she had heard her mother say that he was. He was their family doctor. Mr. Walden was over by the little stage. Mrs. Bunson was at a table near the stage, talking to some of the guests. She would know if Dr. Renner was at the reception. Emily walked quickly to the back of the room.

"Mrs. Bunson, there's a girl upstairs who's hurt, and we need to get a doctor!" Emily panted. "Is Dr. Renner here?"

"What happened?" Mrs. Bunson asked, turning around.

"I said there's a girl upstairs, and she's—"

A loud, screeching wail ripped through the room. The wailing pulsed over and over.

"What's that?" Emily yelled above the noise.

"I don't know," Mrs. Bunson shouted back.

"It's some kind of alarm, I think," a man sitting at the table yelled at the others. "We'd better get out of here. There could be a fire."

"Fire?" Emily yelled in surprise. "I don't smell any smoke."

"Fire alarm!" someone shouted. "Get out!"

There was pandemonium in the room. All the people who had been gathered in the reception hall poured out into the lobby.

"Fire alarm!" one of the caterers shouted. "Get out, quick!"

"Don't panic!" another yelled. "Remain calm!"

Emily felt a wave of fear rise up in her since she was at the back of the room. She joined the mob of people rushing for the doors. In the hall, Rod Williams, the museum guard, was directing traffic.

"Use the stairs, use the stairs!" Rod shouted to people.

"They're safer."

Emily found herself inside the stairwell again. Only this time she was going up and going much more slowly because of all the people trying to leave. The noise of the alarm was even louder in the stairwell. As she got to ground level, people from above were coming down the stairs. She had to wait to get out the door. People were shoving and pushing and shouting. Emily tripped and almost fell. For a moment, she felt like she would be trampled by a human stampede. The alarm screeched loudly.

Finally, she burst through the door into the little hallway in front of the elevators. She ran into the main room of the museum. Confused children and adults were shouting as they lined up at the front doors. It looked like a big human traffic jam.

"Emily!" a voice shouted. She turned her head in the direction of the shout. Josh waved his arms from across the room. Emily pushed her way through the crowd to get to him.

"I was looking for you," Josh shouted above the pulsing alarm. "The other kids got out right away. But now there are too many people at the front door. There's another exit out the back, I think."

"Let's try it," Emily shouted back, trying not to show that she was scared. The two children ran toward the rear of the museum. They passed through three big rooms. At the back of the last big room was a hallway. The big room was empty except for Wade Wyoming, standing in the corner near the hallway.

"There's an exit at the end of the hall," Wade shouted. Emily and Josh ran by the big football player. An emergency door stood open at the end of the little hall. Beyond the door was freedom and safety.

"Let's go!" Josh yelled. He and Emily ran outside. The sky looked even darker, as if it might rain. Lightning flashed in the distance. The alarm kept wailing and wailing as the wind picked up. Even outside it sounded loud. They were at the rear of the museum behind some big air conditioners.

"What a horrible noise." Emily poked her fingers in her ears as if trying to pull out the screeching sound.

"I didn't smell any smoke or see any signs of fire, did you?" Josh asked.

"Nope," Emily replied. "The alarm system sure works well. And loud."

As soon as she spoke, the alarm suddenly cut off. The silence seemed so strangely sweet and soothing. She rubbed her ringing ears. "Finally."

"Let's go around to the front," Josh said. "Maybe we can find out what's going on. Maybe it was another false alarm."

By the time they walked around to the front of the art museum, a big fire engine was already pulling into the parking lot, its siren wailing. Hundreds of people were out on the sidewalk and lawn, talking and pointing at the museum.

The last of the people inside pushed out the big front doors just as the firemen came running up the steps. They were met by two museum guards. While the firemen and the guards talked on the steps, other firemen ran inside. Emily saw another guard come out and talk to the fireman. Another fireman wearing a bright yellow rubber coat ran up the steps. As soon as Emily saw the coat, she thought of Astrid.

"I wonder where Astrid is?" Emily asked.

"Astrid?" Josh repeated.

"Before the alarm went off, she was hurt. I forgot about

her in all the commotion."

"She was the one who screamed? How was she hurt?"

Emily quickly told him about seeing the unconscious girl by the elevators. Josh's eyes widened as the story unfolded.

"I was downstairs looking for Dr. Renner when the fire alarm went off," Emily said.

"That girl sure has her share of problems," Josh said, shaking his head.

"There she is." Emily pointed to a group of people underneath an oak tree out on the front lawn. A fireman was with the group. Astrid was sitting up and talking to the fireman. Emily ran toward the group. Astrid noticed Emily and Josh as they got closer. The fireman touched Astrid's neck carefully. A huge first-aid kit was opened up beside him. It reminded Emily of her father's fishing tackle box, only this was filled with bandages, bottles, needles and other medical supplies. A campus policeman was talking to Astrid. He was an older man, slightly balding on the top. He held a clipboard. Emily noticed that someone had wiped the blood away from Astrid's nose.

"You'll probably get a bruise," the fireman said. "You don't feel dizzy or faint? No spots in front of your eyes?"

"No, I'm just kind of sore," Astrid said.

"You have a pretty good bump on the side of your head," the fireman said, touching it gingerly. Astrid winced in pain as he touched it.

"So you were just leaning against the wall beside the elevators?" the campus guard asked.

"Yeah," Astrid said. "I was just waiting there."

"Waiting for what?"

"I was waiting for some friends." Astrid looked uneasily

into Emily's face but didn't add anything else.

"Then what happened?"

"I already told you once."

"Just for the record, Ms. Flacker," the policeman said. "I've got to make my report."

"Report?" Astrid asked in disgust. "I just wish you'd catch the guy."

"We can't catch him unless we know what happened," the policeman said. "Please cooperate."

"I am cooperating," Astrid replied quickly. "I just don't know what else to say. I was standing there near the door. It opened. I thought it was just someone coming out of the stairs. The next thing I knew someone had his arm wrapped around my neck and was pulling me back into the stairwell. I screamed and bit down on the arm. He threw me into the door frame, and I hit my head. Everything just went dark. When I woke up I was outside on the lawn with an aching head. That's all I remember."

"Did you notice any details about your assailant, like the color of his clothes?"

"He wore long sleeves," Astrid said. "I didn't bite a bare arm."

The policeman frowned. He tapped his ink pen on the clipboard. "I wish we had more information. That's not very much to go on."

"I wish I could tell you more," Astrid said. "It all happened so fast."

"Are you sure it was a man?" Emily asked with concern.

"Yes," Astrid said. "When I bit him, he grunted in a way that sounded like a man."

"Do you have any idea why anyone would do this to you?" the policeman asked.

"No," Astrid said softly. She looked down. No one knew what else to say.

Four firemen came out of the museum and stood on the steps talking. One of them held up a small bullhorn and began to address the crowd.

"There is no fire, folks," the fireman announced from the front steps of the museum. "Someone pulled an alarm in the stairwell. We've checked out the building thoroughly, and there's no reason why you can't go back inside."

"A false alarm," the policeman muttered. "Wouldn't you know it? That's the fourth time. Well, I guess it's better than having a real fire. It's a wonder no one got hurt getting out of the building. I wonder why someone would do something like that?"

"We've had kids pull alarms at schools," the fireman said, closing up his medical kit. "One time a kid did that to get out of taking a test. He was scared he was going to flunk his geometry test. Can you imagine all that ruckus over a silly test?"

"There were lots of kids in there today," the old policeman said. "Probably one of them. Kids these days!"

"What if it wasn't a kid?" Emily asked suddenly.

"Why would you think that?" the policeman asked.

"Because of Astrid," Emily said. "The fire alarm went off soon after she was attacked. Her attacker was most likely in the building still. She was hurt right by the stairs, and the alarm was pulled in the stairwell, they said. He must have known people would start looking for him. What if he pulled the alarm?"

"Yeah," Josh said excitedly. "That would have been a great way to get out. Just pull the fire alarm and cause a bunch of confusion. The building had to clear out, and he could sneak out with everyone else."

The policeman looked closely at Josh. He smiled.

"That's not a bad idea, son," the older man said.

"Emily thought of it," Josh replied, pointing to his sister.

"I'll tell the chief," the fireman said. "You know, it could be true. The other three false alarms were caused by some bug in the computer system, like a power surge or something. This was definitely a pulled alarm."

"Swell." Astrid patted her sore head. "I'm attacked by a clever mugger who got away. Somehow that doesn't make me feel too good. He's still out there running around. What if he comes after me again?"

"I doubt if he'd try it twice." The policeman stood up. "These guys are cowards at heart. Since he knows you bite, he'll probably pick on someone he thinks he can overpower."

"I wish I had done a lot more than bite him," Astrid said bitterly.

"You were lucky," the fireman said. "You distracted him and got away."

"Somehow I don't feel very lucky," Astrid said. She winced as she stood up.

"Let's go over to the chief and tell him what happened to this young lady," the fireman said to the policeman. Then he said to Astrid, "Are you all right now? Do you feel well enough to come with us?"

"I guess," Astrid said without enthusiasm. She looked silently at Josh and Emily. The two men walked away.

"Are you coming?" the policeman called, looking back.

"Yeah," Astrid called out. Then she turned to Emily and Josh. She spoke softly. "I still need to talk to you. I also have your money. Please help me. I think that whoever grabbed me in the museum has my computer."

"What?" Emily asked. "Why do you think—"

"Ms. Flacker, the chief is waiting!" the policeman yelled.

Then the fireman went back and offered Astrid his arm to make sure she was steady as they walked to catch up with the other man. They all walked over to the fire engine that was still sitting in the parking lot.

"I wonder why she thinks the person who grabbed her has her computer?" Emily asked. Josh shrugged his shoulders and shook his head.

"Who knows?" Josh said. "The more I hear, the more confused I get. If she thought that, why didn't she tell the police? Something doesn't make sense here."

Rebecca and Billy Renner ran up to Emily and Josh. Rebecca was smiling.

"We've got to get back inside and get ready to play," Rebecca said quickly. "They're continuing the reception, and it will be time to play soon."

"I almost forgot," Emily said. A jolt of fear jabbed through her insides. She tried to shake it off, but her stomach knotted.

Emily followed her brother and friends toward the big museum steps. People were streaming back inside. Emily was the last in line as they went through the big doors.

At the elevators she saw a red fire alarm on the wall. She looked at it longingly. For a moment she wished there *had* been a fire, just a little one that didn't cause any real damage, but was just enough to cancel the reception. But her wishes faded as the elevator doors opened. She stepped inside. The elevator began going down. Emily felt like she was dropping to her doom.

Chapter Five

# The Performance

The reception room was filled with the noise of people talking. Everyone was more excited than usual because of all the commotion surrounding the false fire alarm. People returned to their tables to finish eating. The food was colder, but it didn't seem to dampen anyone's appetite.

Emily and Josh joined the others at the little stage in the far corner of the room. All the children except Emily were excited. The false alarm was news enough, but when Josh told them about Astrid, their eyes really widened.

"You helped her break in to a fraternity house?" Julie Brown asked Emily.

"Well, she sort of sneaked in. She didn't really *break* in." Emily saw the surprised look on Julie's face.

"That's right," Josh added. "She didn't tell us beforehand."

"It's spooky that someone grabbed her like that," Billy said. "Especially right here in the museum."

"I wonder if it was the same person who set off the alarm," Carlos Brown said as he pulled the cover off his keyboard.

Emily sat down in her chair on the stage, unpacked her flute case and put her flute together. She placed her music on the stand and then looked at Mr. Walden. She knew she was in trouble as soon as she saw his face. He was beaming and bragging to Mrs. Bunson about the group.

"We'll be ready to play whenever you wish," Mr. Walden said. Mrs. Bunson smiled sweetly and went up to the long front table with the microphones.

"Ladies and gentlemen, we do have very special entertainment scheduled for our program," Mrs. Bunson said kindly. "Hopefully we'll be able to make it through our program and meal without any more false alarms."

The crowd laughed. Emily's music slid off her stand suddenly. She jerked her arm forward to stop it, knocking over her whole music stand, which fell with a great clatter. Everyone in the room looked over at the stage. Emily's face was bright red as she hopped out of her chair to pick up the stand and fallen music.

Mrs. Bunson kept speaking at the microphone as Emily rapidly picked up the sheets of music. The other children watched her. Julie offered to help, but Emily refused. Her face was still red when she got everything back in order.

"And to add to your dining pleasure, we will be graced with good music from some of the talented children of Springdale," Mrs. Bunson said. "Mr. Avery Walden is the conductor of the group."

The crowd applauded. Mr. Walden stood up and smiled.

"The musical selections we will be playing are listed in your program notes," Mr. Walden said with a big smile. "We hope you enjoy them." He turned back toward the group. All the children's eyes were on him and on their music at the same time. He waved his arms and the music began.

The first piece was easy because they had performed it several times before. The composition was something Mr. Walden had written himself that he called "Nature's Dance." It reminded Emily of deer and other wildlife skipping through the woods and playing in cool streams while breezes blew gently through the trees. She was always a little nervous when performing in public, especially before such a large gathering where she didn't know many people in the audience. But as Emily played, she began to feel more at ease.

Normally she was proud of the way they played. She enjoyed performing as a part of the group. Practicing alone on her flute wasn't nearly as much fun, and that's why she found it harder to do. She especially found it hard to practice when she knew she could be having more fun on the computer. The flute all by itself was a pretty instrument, but she greatly preferred to be playing with others. The sound was so much fuller and more pleasant than just a single instrument playing along on its own. The harmony made all the difference. The people at the tables were enjoying the music. She could tell by the expressions on their faces after the piece.

The group breezed through the next three pieces without a snag. Mr. Walden was beaming. Emily knew they were doing well. She looked at the crowd. They were still enjoying the music. At the back of the room she saw familiar yellow-blond hair. Astrid was standing in the doorway, watching the musicians. Emily wondered how long Astrid had been there.

"Our final piece is by Mozart," Mr. Walden announced to the crowd. Emily placed her flute up to her lips and took a deep breath.

"I'll sail through this like the rest," she told herself. "Then we'll be done and this whole thing will be over. But I promise I will practice more the next time. I don't ever want to come to a performance again and not be totally prepared."

All the children waited for Mr. Walden's direction. He waved his arm and the music began. Emily came in about a half note too late. She blinked and tapped her foot, trying to get back into the rhythm. She was okay for a few bars, but then the tempo picked up and notes seemed to come faster. Not only that, but for some reason the notes looked very strange. She recognized them and knew that she had played them before, but her fingers suddenly felt heavy and awkward. The other children sailed along, but Emily began missing notes. Josh looked at her out of the corner of his eye, and so did Julie. Emily frowned and stared harder at her music. She could feel her face beginning to turn red.

When it came time to play the next page, she felt totally lost. Over her music stand she could see Mr. Walden looking at her with puzzled eyes. He was conducting all of them, but he kept glancing in Emily's direction as she missed more and more notes.

The section where she and Rebecca played the flute and cello together was coming up. This wasn't exactly a solo, but the flute was supposed to carry the melody, and it would definitely be heard above the low, sweet strings of the cello.

The notes were blurring by too fast. Emily felt sure Mr. Walden was waving his arms quicker and picking up the tempo. The room suddenly seemed very hot. Emily's hands felt moist and clammy, and a drop of sweat began rolling down her forehead. The drop of sweat rolled into her right eye just as the other instruments stopped playing. Mr. Walden was looking right at her.

Rebecca sawed away gracefully on her cello, and Emily tried to come in at the right bar, but when she played, the flute sputtered feebly. She was playing the right fingering and technically the right note, but because she was nervous her lips were in the wrong position, just enough to make the note sound bad. To her, it sounded like the loudest, worst-played note in the history of music. She was sure that not only everyone in the room heard it, but probably everyone in the whole museum. To her, the breathy sputter sounded even louder than the fire alarm. She almost expected everyone in the crowd to jump and run out of the room, just as she wanted to do at that instant.

She squinted at her music and tried to avoid Mr. Walden's eyes. She hit the next few notes on target, but then sputtered again and again. She frowned and more sweat dripped into her eyes. Several bars of arpeggios were coming up like white-water rapids in a raging river. Emily could feel the dread in her stomach growing. She was totally lost when she hit the series of rapid, light notes. Her flute had suddenly turned into a heavy, crude crowbar, and no music would come out of it. She blew and tried to make the delicate fingerings, but she felt like she was wearing mittens. She had overturned in the rapids and stopped playing entirely by the last few bars. Rebecca gracefully continued. The other children tried not to look at Emily, but she could feel them staring. Mr. Walden looked at her with concern. She was sure the whole room was staring at her and noticing every missed note.

Emily tooted a few more times. The others joined in, but Emily could not play. By now tears were streaming down her face, and she couldn't see the music. The others played louder as the piece came to a crescendo, the notes weaving in and out. Emily held the flute up to her lips as if she was playing, but she wasn't even blowing. She wished the flute were big like the cello so she could hide behind it. The tempo increased, the music got very loud, then suddenly stopped. It was over. The people in the audience clapped loudly. Emily looked down at her lap, trying to hide her tears.

After the clapping died down, the people kept eating and the room filled with conversation. Emily kept staring at her lap, afraid to look up because she didn't want to face her friends. She especially didn't want to face Mr. Walden. She glanced up. He was talking to Mrs. Bunson. Then he turned back to the group.

"A good performance," he announced to the group, but he wasn't beaming like he usually did when they played really well. But of course they hadn't played well on the last piece, and Emily knew why. All of them knew why. No one said a word. Emily still had tears running down her cheeks. She laid her flute on her lap and hastily grabbed her music. She shoved the pages back into her folder. She rapidly pulled her flute apart, stuck it into its case and then folded up her music stand. Then as fast as she could, she got up to leave while all the other children busied themselves putting away their music.

She felt like a whole hard-boiled egg was stuck in her throat. She coughed. She had never messed up in a performance before. Mr. Walden was disappointed, and that was the worst thing. Not only had she let the group down, but she had let him down.

Mr. Walden stepped over to her as she was leaving, and the two of them walked away from the stage. She slowed down and looked at Mr. Walden's shoes through her tear-stained eyes.

"What happened, Emily?" he asked softly.

"I, uh, guess . . ." Emily stammered. "I don't know."

"I see," Mr. Walden said seriously. "Did you not have time to practice?"

"No, I . . . uh . . . don't know," Emily said. "I . . . uh . . . uh . . ."

"If we don't practice, we cheat ourselves, and we hurt the whole group, Emily," Mr. Walden said seriously. "I know that I've been gone, and we've missed rehearsals, which is not the way I like to do things. But I assumed that since we've performed all these pieces before we could overcome that deficit. You must know I'm disappointed about the way we performed the last piece. I thought we would all be ready. We depend on each other to know our parts."

"Uh-huh." Emily's voice cracked as she nodded her head up and down. Tears were dripping down like a leaky faucet. Mr. Walden had never said that he was disappointed in the way that they had played. Emily wished she could disappear into a hole in the floor and be totally covered over. By this time the two of them had stopped walking.

The silence was broken when Billy Renner ran over. He was his usual chipper self. "Good show!" he said happily to both of them. Then he turned to Emily. "What happened on the last piece? You didn't sound very good. Are you sick or something?"

"No!" Emily burst into tears and ran to the door. She was crying even harder by the time she got all the way outside the museum.

# Chapter Six

## Tears and Tears

Emily ran and ran across the campus lawn, past buildings and sidewalks, past statues and fountains. She kept running until she came to her favorite cluster of trees. The trees were near the building where her father taught his classes and also had his office. Old cement benches sat patiently beneath the trees as they had for over fifty years. A small fountain and pool of water was in the center of the circle of trees. A few lily pads floated on top of the dark pool. A dragonfly darted above them.

Emily sat on one of the cement benches and wiped her red eyes. She felt very soggy. The front of her blouse was covered with wet splotches. She was glad that all the benches were deserted. She didn't want anyone to see her cry.

"I let everyone down," Emily lamented to herself. "They all hate me for messing up. Josh will tell them why I missed practice. Then they'll really hate me. They may kick me out of the group."

Tears began to fall again. She looked out over the little pond. Several small splashes marked the dark water as rain sprinkled lightly. None of the rain reached her because she was under the covering of the tree branches. Thunder grumbled in the distance like an old man angry at the world.

Emily rubbed her face with her hands. She wished she had a tissue to wipe her nose and eyes. She checked her pockets, but all she had was loose change and two one-dollar bills.

"Need one of these?" a voice asked. Emily jerked her head up. Astrid looked down with a concerned frown. She held out a white tissue. "I have a few left over. The fireman gave me some for my bloody nose."

"Thanks." Emily took the tissue and blew her nose a few times. Being able to breathe made her feel better.

"You can run really fast," Astrid said with a smile. "I had a hard time keeping up with you. I'm glad you came here. This is one of my favorite spots on campus."

"Me too," Emily said.

"I come here to think and read when the weather is good."

"I read here sometimes, too, when we are on campus visiting my dad. His office is in that building right over there."

"Yeah, I know."

"I'm glad he and my mom missed our performance. They'd be really disappointed."

Her eyes filled with tears again, especially as she remembered how Mr. Walden had said that he was disappointed. She had never known she could feel so bad about something. Astrid was quiet. She sat down and patted Emily on the back. Emily burst into tears again.

"I messed up so badly and let everyone down," Emily wailed. Astrid put her arm around Emily's shoulders and squeezed. Emily turned and buried her face in the older girl's shoulder and sobbed even harder. Astrid patted Emily on the back of the head.

Astrid was glad that Emily couldn't see that her own eyes were wet. "It wasn't that bad," Astrid said softly after Emily's sobs subsided a bit. "I heard you guys play three pieces, and you sounded really good on the first two. I was real impressed. When I was your age I knew hardly anyone who could play music like that."

"But I was awful on the last piece," Emily said. "I goofed up."

"Well, they will forgive you, won't they?" Astrid said. "Everyone can have a bad day and goof up. I thought that's what you Christians did. I mean, when one of you falls down, you're supposed to help him back up, aren't you?"

"Yeah, I suppose." Emily sniffled and lifted her head off Astrid's shoulder and saw that it was wet. "I'm sorry, I got you all wet."

"It's going to rain on us anyway," Astrid said with a smile. The rain was now falling harder around them. "Why don't we go inside the engineering building and get a soda before we get soaked?"

"Okay," Emily said. They walked under the trees to avoid the rain. From the last oak tree, Astrid ran across the lawn toward the engineering building. Emily was close behind. Just as they reached the door, lightning flashed and thunder crashed. All at once, sheets of rain fell from the sky.

Inside the building, Astrid led the way to the snack room that was on the first floor. There were soda and snack machines, a few tables and chairs and a couch. A pay phone hung on the wall by the door. There was no one else in the room. Emily looked through the window. Everything was wet and gray as the rain poured in a dull roar.

"We just missed getting a real bath," Emily said, watching the rain fall even harder. The power and majesty of the storm gave her a sense of awe. Lightning flashed again, and she backed away from the window.

"What do you want?" Astrid asked as she surveyed the choices on the soda machine.

"Root beer," Emily said.

"Two root beers," Astrid said. She fed the money into the machine. She gave Emily a can and kept one for herself. She sat down at a table, and Emily joined her.

"How did you know I'm a Christian?" Emily asked after taking a sip of root beer.

"The newspaper article that I read about the Home School Detectives mentioned your church. Besides, everyone on campus knows your dad is a Christian. He's not preachy, but he is very open about what he believes. He's one of the best professors I've ever had. And he's real helpful. Not all Christians are like that. Some people say they're Christians, but they still treat you like dirt. But your dad is different. He's gone out of his way to help me several times."

"He's a good dad," Emily agreed.

"I think he'd even understand if you goofed up a little at your performance," Astrid added, taking a sip of her root beer.

"I hope so." Emily's voice cracked. She appreciated the blond girl trying to cheer her up, but Astrid didn't know the real reason *why* she played so badly. There was a difference between making a mistake and not practicing enough.

"If it were my family, it would be different," Astrid said. "I've messed up, and they hardly want to talk to me. I'm the black sheep in my family."

"Why do you say that?" Emily wanted to ask Astrid about what Wendy and Wade had said, that Astrid had been in jail.

"We had a hard time getting along after my mom and dad divorced," Astrid said. "Everybody just got angry at each other, and things fell apart. But the worst thing happened when I got arrested for computer hacking a few years ago. I broke in to some secured systems. I was curious to see if I could do it. Well, I found out I could. I should have stopped, but they caught me. I didn't mess up any files or steal anything, but it was still a felony. I knew it was wrong. I just didn't think I'd really get caught. I didn't go to a prison, but I was locked up in the county jail a few nights, which was long enough for my family to disown me. They acted like I had practically murdered someone. But they had already stopped caring before then anyway. Getting arrested was just the last straw for them. I haven't been home in over a year. They never call and don't want to see me. I don't really want to be around them either. I still have to go see a parole officer."

"Oh," Emily said with surprise. Astrid seemed very open about what had happened.

"Does that surprise you?"

"I guess not. I mean, I already heard you got in trouble for hacking."

"Did your father tell you?" she asked in surprise.

"No," Emily said. "He never tells us stuff like that about his students."

"Then who told you?"

"Well, I don't know if I should say," Emily said slowly.

"Wendy Phillips," Astrid said flatly. "I saw her at the museum. She was watching me and giving me dirty looks. She doesn't like me. Did she tell you I got arrested?"

"Well . . . yeah," Emily said uncomfortably. "How did she know?"

"I talked about being arrested at the church group that she's a part of on campus," Astrid said with an edge to her voice. "I was hoping the other students wouldn't talk about it. I mean, they said that stuff we shared would be confidential. I guess I shouldn't be surprised."

"You went to the campus church group?" Emily asked.

"Yeah," Astrid said. "Your dad told me about it. I decided to check it out."

"You went to the group Mark and Susan Buckman lead?"

"That's the one. I visited a few times."

"You did? Mark and Susan are a part of our church. Did you like it?"

"It wasn't bad. Mark and Susan are good folks, like your dad. Some of the other students are okay. Some I wouldn't trust any farther than I could throw them, like Wendy. But I was feeling bad about some stuff and wanted to . . . well, you know, pray. Only I don't know much about praying, like how you do it. I didn't grow up going to church. So I visited the group. They asked me to share about my problems. I knew I was taking a chance when I talked about being arrested. But they said it was okay and that people in the group would keep it confidential, like they wouldn't blab it to everyone. So much for that. I wonder who else Wendy told."

"Are you a Christian?" Emily asked.

"No, I don't think I'd say that the way you mean it. I'm thinking about God and stuff, though. It takes me a long time to make decisions. Especially decisions about something that important. I don't want to say I'm going to do something and not follow through. Like if I decided to become a Christian, I wouldn't want to do it halfway. I don't want to say I believe in God, but then live my life like I don't. If I was a Christian, I'd want to be like your dad or the Buckmans. I'd want to be the kind of Christian where I could look at myself in the mirror each morning and respect myself. I've known some people who told me they were Christians, and I never would have believed it from the way they acted. I don't know what God thinks about that kind of people, but personally I don't want to pretend to be something that I'm not. I don't want to live a lie or be a fake around people."

"I don't blame you. I don't either." Then Emily remembered how she had faked her music practice. Her own words seemed to cut right through her heart. Emily felt embarrassed. Suddenly she realized that she didn't want Astrid to know about her own faked practices. "Of course, you can't do everything perfectly just because you're a Christian," Emily said, trying to make herself feel better.

"Of course not. No one is perfect. Anyone can goof up and make mistakes, as you did today on that last piece. You got nervous, and then you didn't play as well, and that can happen to anyone. But it's another thing to do something wrong and try to cover it up or pretend you aren't responsible or that it doesn't matter. That's when you cross over into being a liar. When the police came to my door to arrest me for hacking, I pretended I didn't know what they were talking about. But I felt so guilty. I knew I was lying. They kept asking me questions, and I finally confessed. In a way, it felt really good to get it off my chest. It feels bad to be a liar."

"Oh," Emily said softly. Inside, she felt turmoil over whether to kept silent or to speak up. She knew that Astrid misunderstood why she had played badly at the reception. Part of her wanted to let Astrid keep believing it was just because of nervousness. But another part of her felt that she needed to correct Astrid's misconception. Emily groaned as she thought about it. Her insides were churning. Finally it seemed as if she had to speak. "Well . . . you know . . . I have something to confess, sort of . . . "

"You?" Astrid asked with a smile. "What did you do, rob a bank?"

"No, of course not," Emily replied seriously. She took a deep breath. "You think I messed up on the Mozart piece because I was nervous. But that wasn't really it. I messed up because I hadn't practiced enough. I pretended I was practicing for the last few weeks, but really I played a tape recording of me playing my flute so it sounded like I was practicing. While the tape was playing, I was on the computer looking at stuff on the Internet and World Wide Web."

"You faked your practices so you could go surf the Net?" Astrid asked with surprise.

"Yeah," Emily said softly. "I kept thinking I'd catch up later, like practice real hard at the end of the week or something, but I kept putting it off. I just fooled myself. I should have known the music we were playing today. We've performed that piece before. I knew I needed to practice more. I had time. I just wasted it. That's what makes it so awful. I let everyone down. I thought I could fake my way all the way through. Instead, I just faked out myself."

Emily looked down sadly at her root beer. Her eyes got wet again, but she felt like she was out of tears. She was afraid of what Astrid was thinking.

"I see," Astrid said softly. "You could have fooled me."

"I know. But I didn't want to fool you. You had the wrong impression about what happened. I just . . . I don't know. I don't want you feeling sorry for me for the wrong reason."

"I don't feel sorry for you." Astrid looked at Emily carefully. "You're admitting why you made a mistake. You're taking responsibility for doing something wrong. That's just like your dad. He admits it before the whole class when he makes a mistake."

"Really?" Emily asked.

"Sure." Astrid's eyes suddenly got shiny wet. She looked down at the floor. "Your Daddy-o would understand perfectly."

"Daddy-o?" Emily asked in surprise. "Did Daddy tell you about how we contact each other when we want to chat on the computer?"

"No," Astrid said softly.

"Then how did you know I called him Daddy-o?" Emily asked. "No one knows that but him. Not even Josh knew about it. In fact this morning he was asking me about it. I was trying to chat with my dad this morning on the computer, but he didn't respond."

"That's because he wasn't on-line," Astrid said sadly.

"Of course he was. I know how to check and see when he's on, and it showed that he was there, he just didn't chat back."

"He wasn't there."

"How do you know?" Emily demanded.

"Because it was me."

"You? How could it be you? Did he let you log on under his name? Did he give you the password to his account?"

"No."

"Then how could you have been on?" Emily asked in confusion. "Daddy has a professor's account and privileges on the university system. You couldn't get on there in his name unless you used his password or unless he . . . " Emily knew that all the personal computers on campus were linked together by a mainframe computer. To get access to the mainframe each person had to use his or her own account and special code or password. Still she was bewildered.

Emily's mouth dropped open. She looked at Astrid in amazement. The girl with the wild blond hair looked down at the table. A drop of water fell on her hand. Then another and another. It took Emily a moment to realize that Astrid was crying.

"You mean, it was you I sent the message to this morning?" Emily asked.

"Yeah," Astrid replied. "I was logged on the system in his name when you tried to connect with your dad this morning. That's how I knew what time to look for you at the museum today. I saw that message to your dad."

"How in the world did you get on Daddy's account? You couldn't do that unless . . ."

"I broke in." Astrid's voice cracked as she wiped her eyes. "They don't call me Flacker the Hacker for nothing."

Astrid looked down at her hands again. Emily's mouth hung open. She felt like she did the time she came out of the toy store in Springdale and discovered that her bike was gone and then realized that it had been stolen. It had taken her over a day to accept the fact that someone had actually stolen something of hers. Emily looked at Astrid with surprise. Outside, the rain beat against the window and the wind whipped the trees. Flacker the Hacker began crying again.

# Chapter Seven

# Computer Break-in

Emily watched Astrid cry. She wasn't sure what to do. She had been feeling so bad about herself and her own feelings. Now she was wrapped up in someone else's problem once again. Astrid wiped her eyes with her black sleeve. She pulled a tissue out of her pocket and blew her nose. Then she looked at Emily and waited. Neither girl spoke for a long time.

"You were really able to break in to my father's computer account?" Emily asked.

"Yeah."

"But why would you do such a thing?" Emily demanded. "That's illegal. He has personal mail on his account. Breaking in to someone's computer account is like breaking in to someone's house."

"He also keeps his exam files stored there," Astrid said softly.

"His exams?" Emily asked in surprise. She frowned since she didn't understand. Then she realized what Astrid was saying. "You don't mean that you were trying to steal Daddy's tests? That would be cheating! You could get into a lot of trouble for that. You could get kicked out of school and . . . and . . ."

"And go to jail. Believe me, I know all about it."

"So you admit you were trying to steal his tests?" Emily asked in shock.

"No. You have to believe me. That's not why I was there."

"Then why did you break in?"

"Because I'm sure there are people who *are* stealing exams. They steal them and the answers so they can sell them to students who have bad grades and want to get better grades. Lots of people will do anything to get a good grade. They'll pay hundreds of dollars for a really important test. Even tests without the answers are very valuable because people know ahead of time what to study for and get the answers on their own. It happens around this campus more than anyone realizes. It's a big business."

"Astrid, did you sell stolen exams? Tell me the truth."

She looked Emily in the eye. Her eyes were wet, but she held her chin up. "I did not steal anything, I promise." Astrid's lips trembled.

"But you haven't told me why you broke in to my father's computer account."

"I was checking his files to see if someone else had stolen the exams. That's all I did. You can check the date and time when something has been opened or changed. I was just looking at that information, the time and dates when files were last used or changed. I didn't look at anything personal."

"But you knew I was trying to use the chat command. You saw the message I sent him. That was personal."

"Well, it's true, I did look at that," Astrid said. "But that was the only personal thing I looked at. I knew it was you because of the name. A window on the screen pops open when someone wants to chat. I didn't respond to that. But then you sent the mail message. When you have mail on the university system, you can see who the letter is from and what time it was sent. When you put the pointer on the box and click the mouse button, a window opens up on the screen with the letter. I did look at your letter. But I didn't try to look at any other mail or any exams."

"Did someone steal my father's tests?"

"I think so. They were accessed this morning."

"Maybe my father was making changes."

"At three o'clock in the morning? According to the directory of his files, someone was looking at everything around that time."

"My father wouldn't have been doing anything at that hour."

"That's what I figure, so I'm assuming that someone downloaded the tests. I bet they stole every one of those exams."

"Do you know who it is?"

"Maybe, but I'm not exactly sure," the blond girl replied. "You see, if they're breaking in, they may be using my computer to do it."

"Your computer?"

"Yeah," Astrid said sadly. "I'm afraid that's why my computer got stolen in the first place. I think someone is using it to break in to accounts and steal exams. I think they're selling exams all over the campus. It's not just your father's account either. When hackers know how, they can break in to the accounts of other professors. They could even alter grades and transcripts if they broke in to the right place. They can mess up all sorts of stuff on the university's system if they know how to break in to the right places."

"You think someone's using your computer to do this? What's so special about your computer?"

"I had some programs stored in my computer, programs that help you hack and get in to systems," Astrid said. "I wrote some of the programs myself. Other programs I got from other hackers. It's real technical stuff, but with some luck the programs will work and you can break in to all sorts of places. I should have erased them all after I got arrested, but I didn't. I don't know why. I just kept them. Now I wish I had gotten rid of them, because I think someone else is using those programs to do bad things."

"Astrid, this is really serious." Emily's forehead wrinkled. "How did you break in to my father's account this morning without your computer?"

"I used a computer at the lab in this building. I was just trying to check different professors. I got lucky in guessing your father's password and got in."

"What's his password?" Emily asked.

"You should know. Your Daddy-o uses your name— Emily. It was a lucky guess on my part."

"Oh. I didn't know. This still doesn't sound right. You told us you wanted your computer back because you had your thesis on it."

"Everything I told you earlier is exactly the truth, I promise." Astrid looked at Emily with wide, intense eyes. "You have to believe me. My thesis is on there, and I need to get it back, just like I said. I just didn't think you guys needed to know the other stuff about hacking and someone stealing tests. I didn't tell you because I was embarrassed about being arrested. I didn't think you'd help me if you knew that. Plus I'm still on parole. I can't tell anyone about breaking in to your father's account because I'd be in really big trouble. I know it's illegal, but I was just checking because I felt desperate to see if my suspicions were true. If the police find out my computer is being used in a crime, it will look even worse for me."

"This is all more serious than I thought," Emily said softly.

"I know. I just want my computer back. I should have gotten rid of those stupid programs, and I should have never told Stryker anything."

"Stryker? Who's Stryker?"

Astrid sighed. Her eyes filled with tears again. She took the already soggy tissue in her hand and wiped her nose again. "This is all such a big mess, and I don't know if someone as young as you will understand."

"It's a guy you were in love with, I bet." Emily looked carefully at Astrid.

"How did you know?" Astrid asked with surprise.

"Just a hunch."

"His name is Danny Stryker, but everyone just calls him Stryker. Like you guessed, he's my ex-boyfriend. I really loved him and thought he loved me. We had computer classes together before, only this semester he's not in school because he was low on money. He has a good job and also plays in a band. But I'm afraid he may be involved in all this."

"Why?"

"Because he's a hacker, only he isn't as good at it as I am. When we first started hanging out together a few months ago, he was real curious about how I did stuff back when I got in trouble. He kept begging and begging me to show him how I used to break in to systems."

"Did he tell you why he wanted to do it?"

"Well, at first he said it would be fun. I hoped he was joking. But then he said he knew people who had asked him if he could get tests and exams. He has a reputation around campus as a hacker. He said he could make a lot of money selling exams. Then he said *we* could make a lot of money working together. I told him I didn't want to have any part of it."

"How did he react when you said you wouldn't help him?"

"He didn't make a big deal out of it," Astrid said. "That's why I thought he wasn't really serious. Then I made a dumb mistake."

"What did you do?" Emily drained the rest of her root beer.

"I showed him some of the hacker programs on my computer, to kind of show off, you know?" Astrid said. "I loved him and wanted to impress him. I wanted him to like me. But that was a horrible idea. He was too impressed and wanted me to give him copies of the programs and show him how to use them. I refused, but he wouldn't take no for an answer. I told him they would only cause him trouble, but he kept insisting and asking. Finally, we had a big fight over it one night, and we broke up."

"Do you think he stole your computer?"

"I didn't think so at first. He couldn't have taken it himself because he was with me the night it got stolen. We were having coffee together at a little shop off campus. He walked me to the door of my dorm room. When I went inside, my computer was gone. He acted just as surprised as I was."

"I thought you said you had broken up?"

"We had broken up, but we got back together a week before my computer was stolen," Astrid said. "When we got back together, he told me he was sorry and that he wouldn't bother me about hacking stuff anymore. He seemed sincere and real sweet. He kept his word too. He never mentioned hacking or any of those things the whole week. Then my computer got stolen. That was five days ago. Then two days later, Stryker just dropped out of sight. He hasn't gone to work. I haven't been able to locate him anywhere. Some friends in his band told me they had seen him at the frat house we were at today. That's why I went in looking around for him."

"What do you think is going on?" Emily asked.

"At first I thought he was just sick or something. Then I got worried about him. He hasn't been to his apartment. His roommate said Stryker was going out of town. Then something happened that made me wonder if he was involved in stealing my computer."

"What?"

"Yesterday I got a phone call from a man who asked me if I would like to make some money. Before I could answer, he told me that he knew I was an expert hacker and that someone with 'my talents,' as he put it, could make a lot of money selling exams."

"What did you say?"

"I just said no and hung up."

"Do you think this man and Stryker are working together?"

"I'm afraid they might be." Astrid's voice cracked. "It seems like a big coincidence to me. They both wanted the same thing. But that's not all. Something else happened when that guy grabbed me at the museum that I didn't mention before."

"What?"

"The person holding me said something that scared me."

"But you told the police that he didn't say anything."

"I lied because I was afraid. The guy who grabbed me said, 'Cooperate like a good little hacker,' as he squeezed my neck. That's when I bit him."

"It wasn't Stryker, was it?"

"No, but I've heard this man's voice before. I'm almost positive it was the same person who called me on the phone yesterday asking me if I wanted to steal exams."

"You need to tell the police."

"But I'm scared." Emily could tell the fear in Astrid's eyes was real. "I've already been arrested once for hacking. If they think I'm doing it again, I'll be in really big trouble. This whole thing is turning into a nightmare. I just want my computer back. I never thought Stryker would act like this. He told me he loved me. Do you think he was just using me?" Astrid began to weep softly again.

Emily wished she knew what to say. The situation did seem like a big mess. Emily looked around the room. Through the open doorway, she saw a shadow on the floor in the hall. Emily frowned. She got up and walked across the room. As she got closer to the door, the shadow moved. Emily stuck her head out the doorway. A man was walking away quickly down the hall. His head was down. He wore a dark blue jacket. His dark hair looked wet. He turned the corner and was gone.

Emily looked down. There were wet footprints on the floor. By two of the footprints were little puddles of water.

Emily stared at the water.

"I think someone may have been standing out here in the hall listening to us," Emily said with concern.

"Who cares?" Astrid listlessly pulled another tissue out of her pocket. She wiped her eyes and blew her nose. She looked down at her hands with bleary eyes. "I make a mess out of everything. Maybe my dad is right. He said I was good for nothing but trouble. He said I'd never amount to anything. I got arrested. Then I fell in love with someone who may be a thief. I am a loser."

"That's not true." Emily walked back over and patted her on the back. "I heard you were real smart. Someone even said you were a genius with computers."

"You can be so smart that you outsmart yourself, you know," Astrid said. "I just don't—"

A phone rang. Emily jumped. Across the room, the pay phone on the wall rang again.

"Should we answer it?" Emily asked.

"Why bother?" Astrid asked, sniffling. The phone rang again and again and again and again.

"That's driving me crazy." Emily walked across the room and picked up the phone. "Hello?" She listened for a moment, then stared in surprise at Astrid. "Someone wants to talk to you."

"To me?" the blond girl asked. "How would anyone know I'm in here? I just walked over here following you. No one knows I'm here."

"May I ask who's calling?" Emily spoke into the phone the way she did at home when she was relaying messages to her mom or dad. She listened for a moment. "It's a man, and he says it's urgent that he talk to you. He said his name is Stryker. He says he knows where your computer is."

# Chapter Eight

# Looking in the Library

Astrid walked over to the phone and took it. She held it up to her ear and paused, clearing her throat. "This is Astrid." Then she listened. "Stryker? *Where* have you been?" She listened some more. She frowned at first, then her face broke into a smile. "You know where my computer is? Really?" The blond girl listened. "Yeah. Sure. Right. I'll be right over. That's great! Wait for me . . . I love you too."

Astrid hung up. She reached over and hugged Emily. She yelped with glee. "That was Stryker. He says he knows where my computer is and that he'll help me get it back. He told me to meet him at the library. He told me he loved me." Astrid ran for the door.

"Wait!" Emily shouted. "Are you sure you should go? I thought you said you didn't trust him."

"He said he was out of town visiting an aunt. I'm going to go meet him." Astrid ran into the hall.

Emily ran after her. She caught up with her at the doors that led outside. "Maybe you should take someone with you. What if it's some kind of trick? I mean, how did he know you were in here talking to me?"

"I don't know, and I don't care," Astrid said. "Stryker told me he loved me. I'm going to get my computer back. If I do that soon enough, this whole thing will be over."

"I think you should take someone with you, like the police."

"No way. I'd get in too much trouble. Besides, he told me to come alone. We can't say anything to the police. If I find out who took my computer, then we can tell them, but not till I get it back."

"Maybe Josh and I should go with you," Emily said urgently. "I don't think you should just rush off by yourself. We could be there with you just in case."

"In case of what?"

"In case there's some kind of trouble or something," Emily replied. "What if your boyfriend is lying?"

"He's not lying. Why would he call me? He told me he loved me. He explained where he's been. Besides, he said to come alone."

"But where are you meeting him?"

"I'm meeting him in the basement of the library, near the magazine area."

"I guess the library isn't too dangerous," Emily said slowly. "It's a public place."

"He told me to hurry." Astrid sailed out the door. "Bye." She turned and ran outside into the gray rain, her feet splashing in the puddles on the sidewalk.

Emily watched, biting down softly on her lower lip. "The museum was a public place, and someone tried to grab her there," Emily murmured to herself. "I think she's making a mistake. Why did she need to go alone?"

Emily walked back down the hall toward the snack room. She paused by the door and looked down at the puddles on the floor. There were wet footprints leading up to the puddles, then wet footprints going away. Someone had been standing there long enough to make puddles. Someone had been eavesdropping on them. Emily felt worried and decided to pray. After about five minutes, she felt like she had to act.

Emily took a deep breath and ran down the hall. She pushed open the big door. The rain was still falling hard. Emily ducked her head as she ran out into the downpour. She cut across the grass and headed toward the museum.

"We'll be closing soon," said the guard at the door to the museum. He was sitting in a chair with a newspaper on his lap. Emily was dripping wet. He looked at her wet shoes and frowned.

"I think my brother and friends might still be downstairs at the reception," Emily said.

"You better hurry. The reception is over, and most of the people have left." The guard went back to reading his newspaper.

Emily ran across the polished stone floor toward the elevators. Her wet shoes squeaked every step of the way. She pushed the buttons and waited. She pulled her little New Testament out of her pocket to see if it had gotten too wet. The edges of the pages were damp and slightly wrinkled, but the plastic cover had kept the book mostly dry. Emily shoved the little book back into her pocket. When the elevator doors opened, she got in and went down two floors. As she got out, Rod Williams, the guard, came out of a door at the end of the hall pushing an empty handcart.

"Looks like you got caught in the rain," he said with a smile.

"Yeah. I'm soaked. Do you know if my brother is still here?"

"Sure. He's been helping me and some of the guys tear down the stage and clear the room. He's a big help. I just put away part of the stage and came back for the rest."

"I thought you were a guard," Emily said.

"Well, if you work for the university, they treat you like a slave, and you do whatever Mr. Bunson tells you," Rod said. Emily wasn't sure if Rod was joking or not. "Mr. Bunson is going to retire next month. Personally I'll be glad to see him go."

Emily walked quickly into the reception room. Rod pushed the empty cart into the room behind her. Most of the people had left. Mr. Bunson was at the front of the room talking to a young man with a white coat. Other young men with white coats were picking up dishes and putting them on carts. Rod and Emily walked over to where the stage had been.

"Your sister's back," Rod said.

Josh was sitting on a chair, reading a book. He looked up quickly. He frowned when he saw Emily. "Where have you been? And why are you all wet? I was starting to get worried. Mr. Walden left. So did the Renners and the Browns."

"I was too embarrassed to stay. Was Mr. Walden really mad?"

"He didn't say a word about it after you left. You goofed up, but it wasn't the end of the world."

"Well, it wasn't you making the mistakes."

"I don't think you had to run out like that, but I guess I'm not surprised. I figured you'd come back. Don't forget that we're supposed to meet Mom and Dad over at Dad's office at eight o'clock."

"I haven't forgotten." Sometimes Emily felt like Josh treated her like a four-year-old.

Rod began stacking sections of stage onto an empty cart. Josh put down his book and helped him. Emily watched them.

"Were the other kids mad?" Emily finally asked.

"I don't think so." Josh grabbed another section of stage. "No one said anything to me. I think they might have been embarrassed. But no one wanted to talk about it. Billy wondered where you went. I told him you'd be okay when you got over being upset."

"I just went over to Daddy's building."

"I thought you'd probably go over there. I tried calling his office, but no one answered. I thought you might be in the lab playing with one of the computers."

"I was down in the snack room talking to Astrid."

"Her again? Why were you talking to her?"

"Astrid saw me leave here, and she followed me," Emily said. "She was real nice to me. Did you know she visited the Christian group on campus? Then she told me more stuff about her stolen computer."

"Oh, boy. Does she want us to help her sneak into some other place?" Josh asked in disgust.

"Don't say that. You've got to hear what she told me. I'm worried about her. In fact I think we need to go check on her. That's why I ran back here. She's over at the library, and she might be in danger."

"In danger at the library?" Josh asked sarcastically. "Is someone throwing books at her?"

Rod laughed with Josh. Together they put another long section of the stage on the cart.

Rod stood up, stretched and said with a smile, "You couldn't get in too much trouble at the library."

"Well, she's the girl who got attacked here earlier near the elevators, just before the fire alarm went off," Emily said. "Who would have thought the museum was a dangerous place?"

"She's a wacko, I think," Rod grunted. "I heard the other guards talking about her. Some of them think she may have fallen down and said all that other stuff just to be dramatic. Or maybe she's loony, you know, full of mental problems. Did you see how many earrings she's got and that weird hair? Plus she's so pale. She doesn't look healthy to me. She could be on drugs."

"You mean they don't believe that she was really attacked?" Emily asked. "What about the lump on her head?"

"She obviously fell," Rod said. "But that doesn't mean that she was attacked. No one saw anyone grab her or anyone run away. I'm not saying she made it up, but she could have. You never know with people like her."

"I think she was attacked, and I think she may be in big trouble," Emily said forcefully. "Listen to what happened."

Emily quickly told her brother and Rod about her conversation with Astrid. The more Josh heard, the more surprised he looked. Even the big guard raised his eyebrows as Emily told them the story.

"And then we got this phone call out of the blue," Emily said. "How would this Stryker guy even know we were in the snack room?"

"Maybe someone told him?" Rod offered.

"I think he may have been listening at the door," Emily said. "I told you I saw the wet puddles on the floor and someone walking away."

"That doesn't prove anything in itself," Josh said. "But she *is* in big trouble if she broke in to Dad's computer account. That's illegal."

"That's just the point," Emily said. "Why would she confess that to me, knowing that I would tell Daddy? She knows it was wrong and that she could get in a lot of trouble. She was just being honest. I think all the stuff she told me is true. I think there are people stealing exams. And I don't think that Stryker guy can be trusted."

"Do you know Stryker?" Josh asked Rod.

"Never heard of him," Rod said, rubbing his chin. "I never heard of that blond girl until today. It sounds to me like she's got a lot of problems. I keep my nose out of other people's problems. I mean, if she's in trouble, it's her own fault for hanging around other troublemakers. That's the way I see it."

"Maybe we should go over to the library and just check on her," Josh said with concern.

"Probably won't hurt to check," Rod said. "I'm going that way myself with the rest of the stage. They keep this stage stored down there in the library basement. We can go together if you want."

"Really?" Emily asked. "That's real sweet of you. I'd rather be with someone older and bigger. You look tough. If this Stryker guy is mean, he'll be afraid of you."

Rod gave a big goofy grin and nodded his head. He smiled at Emily because she was complimenting him. He was proud of his size.

"Yeah, he better be afraid," the big guard said. "I bet her story is just a bunch of phony baloney. But hey, I'm going over there anyway, so it's no skin off my nose. Let me go tell Mr. Bunson where I'm going. He likes to know where all his slaves are at all times. He's real bossy."

Rod went over to Mr. Bunson, who was giving orders to the crew taking down the tables. The two men talked for a few minutes. Then Rod returned.

"Let's go." Rod began pushing the cart toward the elevator. Josh and Emily followed. They went up the elevator to the ground floor. Rod pushed the cart to the front door. The guard got up and opened the door.

"Where are you going?" the guard asked.

"Taking the stage back to the library." Rod quickly pushed the cart outside. Emily and Josh were right behind him.

The rain wasn't falling as hard as it had been, but by the time they got to the library, Josh and Rod were nearly as wet as Emily. Rod pushed the cart to the elevator. All three went down two floors. The elevator bell dinged and the door opened. A woman sat behind a counter straight across from the elevator. She stared at Rod and the wet children. A name plate which said *Beula Hathaway, Periodicals Librarian* sat on top of the counter. Emily recognized her face.

"Is the reception over already?" Mrs. Hathaway asked Rod.

"Yep," Rod said. "Mr. Bunson is making me bring back the portable stage. He knows I'm a museum guard, but here I am lugging around the portable stage like the old days."

"I guess he can't forget how good a custodian you were," Mrs. Hathaway replied. "Everyone is coming in here like soaked rats today. I thought you'd stay out of the rain."

"Well, when Mr. Bunson yells jump, we all jump," Rod growled as he pushed the cart past her.

The main room with all the magazines was off to the left of the elevators. Since Emily and Josh had been to the library many times over the years, they knew where everything was. They walked over to the magazine rack. Rod pushed the cart behind them.

"I don't see them anywhere." Emily looked intently around the room.

"Let me put this over by the storage room, and I'll help you look." Rod pushed the cart over to the far wall and left it by a closed door. Emily and Josh spread out around the room, searching for Astrid. They walked up and down every aisle of magazines and looked in every corner of the room. The last place Emily looked was the girls' bathroom, but it was empty too. She joined Josh and Rod over by the magazine section.

"She's gone," Emily said anxiously.

"I don't see her either," Josh said.

"I wouldn't worry about it," Rod grunted. "She probably came and went already. Not much you can do about that."

Emily walked over to the front desk by the elevators. Mrs. Hathaway looked up. "Do you know who Astrid Flacker is?" Emily asked.

"Of course," the librarian said. "She helped us hook our computers to the university network. We were the last ones to get connected to the central system. She's a whiz when it comes to those machines. The service technicians were having a horrible time. Astrid was down here doing research. She started asking the technicians questions. Within an hour she was telling them what cable went into what socket. She was amazing. In fact she came in a few minutes ago. She's right over there."

Mrs. Hathaway pointed to a chair near the magazine rack. The old woman blinked. "Well, she was right over there," Mrs. Hathaway said. "She must be down here somewhere. I didn't see her leave."

"But we've looked everywhere," Emily said. "She was going to meet a boy named Danny Stryker down here."

"Danny Stryker?" Mrs. Hathaway said grimly. "He hasn't been down here. He's not even a student this semester."

"You know who he is?" Emily asked.

"Of course I know him," the librarian said sharply. "They caught him trying to walk out of here with a whole stack of computer magazines once. He said he just forgot they were in his backpack, but who forgets ten magazines? I know that boy all right, and whenever I see him I watch him like a hawk because he's a thief."

"You're sure you didn't see him down here talking with Astrid?"

"I would remember seeing Danny Stryker," the librarian said. "You have to keep your eyes open around that boy."

"I don't like this," Emily said to Josh. "I'm worried. Where could Astrid have gone? She said she was going to meet Stryker here. She was so excited. Something's not right."

Emily walked around the room quickly once more. But there was still no sign of Astrid Flacker.

# Chapter Nine

# Going Underground

"Are you sure Astrid didn't leave without your noticing?" Emily asked Mrs. Hathaway. Emily tapped her fingers nervously on the wooden counter.

"Well, she may have, but I've been at the desk ever since she came in," Mrs. Hathaway said. "She must have slipped out without me seeing her. But I'm sure she wasn't with that awful Danny Stryker. I would have noticed him come in for sure."

"Thanks," Emily said.

"I better go put the rest of the stage away." Rod walked over to his cart. He took out his keys and opened a door on the far wall. He pushed the cart inside a dark room.

"Let me go help Rod unload those, and you keep looking around," Josh instructed.

Emily nodded. She walked around the whole magazine section again. She checked every study desk, every chair and every aisle. She even checked the restroom once again.

"Still no sign of her?" Mrs. Hathaway asked.

"None." Emily walked over to the storage room to get Josh. She went inside. The room was bigger than she expected. Tables and chairs were stacked around the room. Shelves with books on them were leaning against one wall.

Josh and Rod were carefully taking the sections off the cart and stacking them with the rest of the stage. Emily sighed. At the far end of the room there was a dark hallway. She walked over to take a look. The roof of the hallway was covered with big pipes and black electrical cables. The hallway disappeared off into darkness. On the wall was a light switch. Emily flicked the button.

Light bulbs inside little wire cages lined the ceiling of the hallway. The lights were dingy, but they lit the long dark hallway for a long way, over fifty yards or more before it stopped or turned.

"We're done," Josh called to Emily.

"Yeah." Rod pushed the empty cart. "We better go. Turn off that light switch."

"Where does that hallway go?" Emily asked.

"I'm not sure." Rod reached over and flipped off the light before she could do it. "It's some kind of utility tunnel or something for pipes and stuff. I stay out because there are too many spiders."

"Really?" Emily couldn't tell if the guard was joking or not. He grinned at her, but the way he grinned still made her wonder if he was serious.

"We better get back before that Mr. Bunson has a heart attack. He doesn't like his slaves to catch their breath."

Josh laughed. They followed Rod back to the door. After

he closed it, he locked it with his keys. Josh led the way to the elevator. Rod brought up the rear, pushing the cart.

"Back to the grindstone," Rod said to Mrs. Hathaway as he rolled the cart past her.

He pushed the cart into the elevator. Emily got on last. She looked back at the empty room with a frown. Her mind was racing about what could have happened to Astrid. At the same time, she felt like she was forgetting something. The elevator rose two floors. The bell dinged and the doors opened. They all got off but Emily.

"Now I remember!" Emily said as the others got off.

"You remember what?" Josh asked.

"I forgot to leave my phone number with the librarian," Emily said.

"Why would she want your phone number?" Rod asked.

"I want her to give it to Astrid in case she turns up," Emily said. "I'm going back down. I'll meet you back at the museum."

"Don't be long," Josh warned. "I think you're wasting your time."

"It's worth a try." Emily pressed the button and the doors closed.

Down in the basement, Emily hurried over to the counter. She shivered. She had forgotten her wet clothes in the excitement about looking for Astrid.

"Can I have a piece of scratch paper?" Emily asked. "I'd like to make a note and leave it for Astrid in case you see her."

"Sure." Mrs. Hathaway gave Emily a piece of paper. While Emily wrote, she sneezed. She gave the librarian the note. Mrs. Hathaway handed her a tissue.

"Thanks." Emily wiped her nose.

"Is it still raining outside?" Mrs. Hathaway asked.

"Yes. I guess it doesn't matter. I'm already wet as it is."

"I wonder why he didn't take the tunnel," Mrs. Hathaway said.

"What?"

"Rod usually goes back and forth between here and the museum in the tunnel," the librarian said.

"There's a tunnel that goes to the museum?"

"Tunnels connect almost all the major buildings on campus," the librarian said. "They're utility tunnels for water pipes, computer cables and so forth. If you know where you are going, you can go from one end of the campus to the other completely underground. Rod always comes over here through the tunnel, especially when it's raining."

"He does?" Emily asked.

"Sure," Mrs. Hathaway said. "In fact, I was surprised to see him in those wet clothes. I guess there could be some problem with the pipes, and the tunnel could be blocked off for some reason."

"Blocked off? He told me he doesn't go in there because he doesn't like spiders."

"You think someone as big as Rod would be afraid of spiders?" Mrs. Hathaway asked with a laugh.

"That's what he said."

"When he was a custodian he practically lived in those tunnels," the librarian said with a smile. "He must have been pulling your leg."

"I guess so."

"I'll be sure and give Astrid your note if I see her," the librarian said.

Emily didn't answer, because she was thinking. She ran to

the elevator and pushed the buttons. When the elevator didn't come right away, she decided to use the stairs. She ran up them as fast as she could.

Outside, she kept running. The rain was still falling as she ran to the museum. The same guard sat near the front door, reading his newspaper.

"We're closing in five minutes," the guard said.

"Rod could let us out, couldn't he?" Emily asked.

"He sure could," the guard replied. "He or Mr. Bunson will have to, because I'm going home in five minutes. I don't work overtime."

Emily's wet shoes squeaked as she walked on the stone floor. The big exhibition hall seemed eerily quiet. The elevator doors were open and waiting, so she took it. When she got to the bottom floor, she burst into the hallway. The reception room was off to her left, but she went to the right. At the end of the hallway was a door. A small sign was stenciled on the middle of the door.

*STAFF ONLY*
TUNNEL SYSTEM
*ENTRANCE 19*

Emily turned the doorknob. To her surprise, the door opened. She peeked in. The room was dimly lit. A knot of fear gripped her stomach. Without going in she softly closed the door.

"Josh, you've got to help me on this," she whispered to herself.

Emily turned and walked quickly to the reception hall. Josh was watching Rod and some other custodians load folding chairs onto a long rolling rack. Mr. Bunson stood there watching with his hands on his hips. Emily walked over to the older man.

"Mr. Bunson, does that door out in the hall lead to the tunnel system that's underneath the campus?" Emily asked.

"Why, yes, I believe it does," Mr. Bunson replied. "Why do you ask?"

"Oh, I was just wondering." Emily turned to her brother. "Josh, we need to be going. I've got some phone calls I want to make. It's important."

"Phone calls?" Mr. Bunson asked. "You can use the employee office if you wish. It would be a local call, of course? I could go with you and open the door."

"We can use the pay phone by the front door," Emily said quickly. "I want to call . . . I want to call . . . some neighbors of ours and make sure our ride is coming."

"It's no trouble for me," Mr. Bunson said with a smile. "It would save you a quarter . . . "

"It's only a quarter. Let's go, Josh."

She grabbed her brother by the arm and pulled him toward the door. Mr. Bunson watched them leave. Rod Williams looked up.

"Thanks, Josh!" Rod called from the other side of the room. The guard waved at the two children. Emily smiled and kept pulling her brother's arm until he was out of the room.

"What's gotten into you?" Josh asked as they walked out into the hallway. "Why are you trying to pull my arm off just to make a phone call?"

"I want to call the police," Emily whispered.

"The police?"

"Yes. I think I know what happened to Astrid. But first we have to check something out." In the hallway, she pulled Josh over to the door with the stencil writing that said *STAFF*

*ONLY.* She opened the door and started to go inside.

"That's for employees only!" Josh grabbed his sister's arm.

"I want to look around. We won't bother anything."

"Wait a second." Josh still held her arm. Emily shut the door softly. "Will you tell me what's going on?"

"There's a tunnel in there that leads all the way to the library," Emily said. "In fact, Mrs. Hathaway said the tunnels go underneath the whole campus."

"So?"

"Rod said he never went into the tunnels because he was afraid of spiders," Emily replied. "But Mrs. Hathaway said he used to be a custodian and used the tunnels all the time."

"So, he was kidding you. So what?"

"I don't think he was just kidding. I think he was lying."

"Lying about what?"

"I think he lied about using the tunnels," Emily said. "In fact I know he did. Think about it. The portable stage is stored over by the library basement. How many trips did it take for him to move all the sections of the stage?"

"Three," Josh said. "I helped him load up the cart each time."

"It's been raining all afternoon, but when I came down here, Rod's coat and pants and hair were dry, weren't they?"

"Yeah, I guess you're right."

"That means he didn't go outside, which means he used the tunnel to go to the library except for that last trip with us," Emily said.

"What's your point?"

"Why wouldn't he take us to the library using the tunnel, especially since it was still raining? And why would he lie about it unless he had something to hide?"

"That does seem a little odd. Why do you think he did it?"

"Mrs. Hathaway said she saw Astrid come into the basement of the library, but she never saw Astrid leave. Astrid either slipped out unnoticed, or she left another way."

"You think she went through the tunnels?" Josh asked. "But the door to the storage room was locked from the outside. She couldn't have gone through there, and she wouldn't have a key."

"But what if someone else opened that door?" Emily asked. "What if someone opened that door from the inside and took Astrid out through the tunnels?"

"You think Rod had something to do with it?"

"He came out of the tunnels just as I got here, through this door. Remember? Rod and I came into the room at the same time. He was pushing the cart. He would have been over at the library around the same time that Astrid was there."

"Maybe," Josh said. "But that's kind of thin. I thought she was going to meet her old boyfriend, Stryker. He was the one who called her. She couldn't have mistaken his voice."

"I know, but that fits too. Mrs. Hathaway didn't ever see Stryker come into the magazine room. But what if Stryker came through the tunnels? He could have opened the door, seen Astrid, and then lured her into the storage room. Bingo, they got her!"

"So you think Rod was working with Stryker?"

"Maybe," Emily said. "It's worth checking out."

"I suppose that could explain how Astrid could disappear. But I don't know if you'd convince the police of anything. It doesn't explain why anyone would want to kidnap her. It doesn't explain a lot of things."

"But it's a start. Something isn't right. That's why I want to take a look around in here. Please? Let's just take a quick peek."

"Just a quick one."

Emily opened the door. The room was dark, but Josh found a light switch on the wall and turned it on. Once they were inside, Emily shut the door behind them.

A gray metal desk and chair sat near the door. The far side of the room was lined with gray lockers. Off to the right she saw the opening to a dark hallway. She walked over. At the mouth of the hallway she found another light switch. She hit the light, and the hallway lit up.

"Wow!" Josh said. "That must go over a hundred yards."

"And you can see the openings to other tunnels," Emily said.

"It still doesn't prove Rod had anything to do with Astrid's disappearance."

"But it does prove he's lying about the tunnels for some reason," Emily said. Josh turned off the lights. Emily looked around the room carefully. She walked over to the row of gray lockers. Each locker had a name stenciled on it in black paint.

"There's Rod's locker," Emily said. The door of the locker was slightly ajar. She pulled it open.

"I don't know if you should be doing that."

"There's not much in it anyway," Emily said. A can of deodorant sat on the shelf. A bare metal hanger dangled on a short rod. At the bottom of the locker was a wadded-up gray jacket. She picked it up to put it on the hanger. As she did, she saw something red on the sleeve. Emily looked closer.

"I think this is blood." Emily held it up to the light. On the right sleeve was a slight rip and tiny hole surrounded by a stiff red stain.

"Yeah, it does look like blood," Josh said. "I wonder . . ."

"Astrid's attacker!" Emily almost shouted. "Remember,

she said that when that guy tried to grab her, she bit him hard on the arm. That's why she got away. She could have drawn blood and made him bleed."

"I think you may be right," Josh said. "Let's get out of here and—"

"And what?" a voice said behind them. Mr. Bunson stood in the doorway looking at the two children.

"Mr. Bunson, are we glad to see you," Emily said. "I think we may know who tried to kidnap Astrid Flacker earlier today. We just found this coat in Rod's locker and there's blood on the sleeve. I think that—"

"Yes, I heard what you think." Mr. Bunson nodded his head. "In fact I happened to overhear you two talking in the hall outside just a little while ago, and I was very intrigued. I had heard about you and your friends and your detective work, but I never thought I'd actually get to see you in action. You both are very clever for your age."

"I think it's enough evidence to call the police, don't you?" Josh asked. "I mean I think they would want to ask Rod some questions for sure."

"I don't know. What do you think?" Mr. Bunson asked, only he wasn't talking to Emily or Josh. He turned back to the open door. Rod Williams stepped into view and looked at the two children.

"I don't think I want to answer any questions just yet," Rod said.

"I don't think that would be wise either," Mr. Bunson replied.

The big guard nodded and smiled. He closed the door. The lock clicked. Rod Williams smiled again as he slowly walked toward Emily and Josh.

# Chapter Ten

# The Alarm Goes Off

Emily wanted to scream, but she was too surprised and too scared. Josh seemed very confused for a moment. Rod opened a desk drawer and pulled out a thick roll of gray duct tape. He pulled the end of the tape out almost a yard.

"Put your hands behind your back," Rod said to Josh.

"What are you going to do with us?" Josh said. "You can't—"

"Be quiet, boy, and do as he says!" Mr. Bunson hissed. His face was red with anger. "You snoops have caused enough trouble. I hate complications. I can't believe a couple of kids are interfering with my plans. You two will be sorry you ever stuck your nose into my business."

Josh glared at the two men as he put his hands behind his back. Rod tightly wrapped the tape around and around Josh's wrists. Josh winced in pain as the big man pulled it tighter.

"Now you," the guard said to Emily. He smiled. "I've got a pair of these janitor's handcuffs that are just your size."

"Better do as he says," Josh muttered. Emily reluctantly put her hands behind her back. Rod wrapped the tape around Emily's wrists. She groaned as he jerked her arms.

"Don't you hurt her!" Josh warned.

"What are you going to do about it?" Rod asked with a smile.

"I should bite you like Astrid did," Emily said. For a second, the guard leaned away from the girl.

"I wouldn't try it. That little punk is going to regret she ever bit me. When we're through I'm going to fix her good."

"Quit talking and let's go!" Mr. Bunson exclaimed.

"Go where?" Josh asked. "Why are you doing all this?"

"They're involved in stealing exams, just like Astrid said," Emily accused.

"Come on." Mr. Bunson pushed Emily toward the tunnel. Rod stood behind Josh.

"Let's go, Josh," the guard said. "I don't want to have to hurt you."

Josh nodded. He followed his sister into the tunnel. Rod flipped the switch. The two children and two men walked without speaking. Josh looked over at Emily. She shrugged her shoulders, trying to arrange her arms so they felt more comfortable. But no matter which way she wiggled, it still hurt.

At the first intersection in the tunnel, they turned right. Mr. Bunson led the way.

"Faster, faster," the assistant manager barked at the others.

They turned down another hallway and walked another fifty yards. They turned again and continued walking down another hallway. Finally they stopped at a closed door. Mr. Bunson got out his keys and opened the door. He went inside. Rod pushed Josh and Emily into the room.

"Astrid!" Emily yelled. The girl with blond hair was sitting at a desk across the room. Her eyes were bleary. Her right eye was puffy and an ugly purple bruise marked her cheek. In front of her was a tan notebook computer. Her hands were on the keyboard. A young man with long black hair and a scraggly beard was sitting in a chair next to her holding a revolver. He wore a wet blue jacket. He looked surprised to see Emily and Josh.

"Emily!" Astrid called. "What are you doing here?"

"Yeah, what are they doing here?" the young man repeated.

"We caught them nosing around," the assistant manager said. "They found Rod's jacket with blood on it. They had too many questions and were going to go to the police. We had to stop them."

"The police?" the young man asked. "We've got to work fast. No one is going to worry if Flacker the Hacker is missing. But these kids have parents. They'll be looking everywhere when they don't turn up."

"It couldn't be helped, Stryker," Mr. Bunson said. "We'll worry about them later. Has she figured out how to turn off the alarms or not?"

"She's in, but she says she's not sure about turning off the alarms," Stryker said.

Astrid stared wearily at the screen of the notebook. A telephone line was connected to the side of the small computer. Astrid rapidly tapped the keyboard.

"You need to try harder, young lady," Mr. Bunson said. "I hope you're not stalling."

"I'm trying," Astrid grunted. "Once you get in, there are help windows, actually, but you have to take time to read them."

"You better read fast and hard," Mr. Bunson replied. "I want that alarm turned off. And if you don't, I will do something very painful to your little friends here."

"Don't you touch them!" Astrid spat out. "All they tried to do was help me."

"Then I suggest you get the alarm off soon or your little helpers are going to suffer," Mr. Bunson said.

"Alarm? What alarm?" Emily demanded. "I thought you said they were trying to steal tests."

"Tests," Rod Williams said with disgust. "Tests are a good side business, but it'll take too long to get rich selling tests to all the lazy idiots on campus."

"It's too much risk," Mr. Bunson said dryly.

"I made over three thousand dollars this morning," Stryker said proudly. He scratched his scraggly beard. "That's not too bad. Those fraternity boys couldn't wait to lay their money on the table."

"That's pocket change," Mr. Bunson replied. "I want to make some real money. You have to teach these young people how to think big."

"Yeah, we can retire and live in the Bahamas on this deal," Rod grunted. "I've got my suntan lotion and bathing suits packed."

"What system are you in?" Emily asked.

"The security system at the art museum," Astrid said flatly as she stared at the screen.

"The art museum?" Josh asked.

"They want me to turn off the alarm for the Gutenberg

Bible," Astrid said bitterly. "They're going to steal it."

"Steal it?" Emily asked. "You're going to steal the Bible?"

"A nice retirement present for me and my two loyal helpers," Mr. Bunson said, nodding at Stryker and Rod Williams. "It's worth millions, even if we sell it cheaply."

"But there are only a few copies of the Gutenberg Bible in existence," Josh said.

"Forty-eight, to be exact," Mr. Bunson said with a smile. "Of course you would know that if you were a good student and listened to your tour guide."

"If you steal that copy, and it goes on the market, then everyone will know where you got it because news will spread," Josh said. "No legitimate art collector or auction house would help you. They would turn you in to the police."

"Yes, my boy, you are right," Mr. Bunson said condescendingly. "But fortunately there are many illegitimate art dealers and very rich private collectors who hate red tape and love bargain prices on priceless antiquities. In fact, I already have a buyer who intends to sell it to one such rich collector. You see, one has to learn to be industrious and think big, as I've been telling my young friends here. Since the university saw fit not to promote me according to my talents and cheated me out of my rightful salary, I decided to take matters into my own hands. Only Mr. Stryker here wasn't as talented at breaking in to systems as he claimed. All he could manage was setting off the fire alarms like some dimwitted schoolboy."

"Hey, this stuff isn't like cracking the secret codes on video games," Stryker shot back. He stood up and glared angrily at Mr. Bunson.

"Needless to say, we recruited, shall we say, the campus

expert on hacking, Ms. Flacker," the assistant manager said. "Now hurry up. The museum closed five minutes ago. The van is waiting behind the library, and I'm getting anxious. You either get that alarm off now or I'm going to let Rod think of creative ways to cause pain to this little girl."

Mr. Bunson pushed Emily in Rod's direction. With her arms behind her back, she lost her balance and tripped. She fell to the floor. Her New Testament flipped out of her pocket. Rod leaned over and stuffed the tiny book back into her pocket.

"Don't you hurt her!" Astrid shrieked.

"Then quit stalling and get that alarm off," Mr. Bunson yelled.

Astrid muttered under her breath. She tapped the keys rapidly. She watched the screen. A window on the screen closed and another opened. She typed two more characters. She leaned back in her chair.

"It's off," she said simply.

"Are you sure?" Rod asked. "How can we be sure?"

"Look for yourself." Astrid pointed to the screen. "The Bible is the only exhibit with alarm security. See all those items, Display Number One, Display Number Two, et cetera? All the displays were already off, except the first one. That can only be the Gutenberg Bible."

"Why couldn't you figure that out?" Mr. Bunson said to Stryker.

"The exhibit alarm system is at a deeper level than the fire alarm system," Astrid said. "Plus he probably keyed in the wrong sequence and set off the alarm."

"Three times he set it off," Mr. Bunson snarled. "I was ready to shoot him."

"Hey, I gave it my best shot," Stryker said. "Anyway, I delivered the girl for you like I promised. And we got the alarm off. I see it as a team effort."

"Okay. You two go get the book," Mr. Bunson said. He handed them a gray laundry duffel bag that was lying in the corner. He took Stryker's gun. "Get back here as quick as you can. If I hear the alarm going off, I will use the gun on these three. We'll lock their bodies in a closet down the hall and get them out later. And remember, boys, don't try any ideas of your own. You'd never be able to sell that book without my help and my connections in the world of antiquities."

"Don't you trust us, man?" Stryker asked. "That hurts my feelings."

"I'm just reminding you that we're partners," Mr. Bunson said coldly. The assistant manager turned back to Astrid. He stuck the gun right in front of her face.

"Did you hear me, Ms. Hacker?" Mr. Bunson asked with a sneer. "If I hear one little tweet of an alarm, I'm going to use this gun. We are far below ground level, and no one will hear it. Now are you sure that alarm is off?"

"As far as I can tell," she said flatly.

"Go get that book," Mr. Bunson said. Rod Williams and Danny Stryker left the room. Astrid leaned back in the chair. She gingerly rubbed the black-and-blue mark on her cheek.

"I'm sorry you guys got involved," Astrid said to Emily and Josh.

"We were worried about you," Emily replied. "Are you all right? Your cheek is really bruised."

"I'm okay." Astrid's eyes suddenly got shiny with tears. "But I feel like such a fool. I thought he really loved me . . ."

The girl with a bruise under her right eye began to sniffle.

A teardrop fell from her nose onto her keyboard.

"How touching," Mr. Bunson said. "I must remember to give Mr. Stryker an A for his acting ability. I didn't think he'd ever get you to cooperate. But the boy does have some talent after all. He may not know as much as he claims about computers, but he does have a talent with the ladies. He has a real girlfriend. In fact he has two girlfriends. Of course, I guess he wouldn't tell you that . . ."

Mr. Bunson chuckled softly. Astrid buried her face in her hands and sobbed softly. The man holding the gun looked down at her with contempt.

"What a jerk," Josh said to Mr. Bunson.

"You are a mean person," Emily added. "I hope God can forgive you. I'm not sure I'll be able to."

"I don't really think I'll lose much sleep over that," Mr. Bunson said. "You two might as well sit down and be comfortable while we wait. Don't try anything heroic. If you cause any trouble, I will not hesitate to use this gun."

Josh and Emily sat down. Emily wiggled her hands, but the sticky tape held fast.

"What are you going to do with them?" Astrid asked as she wiped her eyes.

"You should be worried about what we're going to do with you," Mr. Bunson said.

"I'm praying, Astrid," Emily said.

"Me too," Josh said.

"I think I'm learning how to pray myself," Astrid said to Emily. "I didn't know it would take all this for me to learn."

"Shut up!" Mr. Bunson said. "There will be no more talking!"

The next fifteen minutes seemed to take an eternity to

Emily. She was braced in case she heard the noise of an alarm. Mr. Bunson seemed exceptionally calm for a man who was stealing something worth millions of dollars. She prayed harder.

The door suddenly burst open. Rod and Stryker walked in grinning. Rod carried the laundry bag over his shoulder as if it held a sack of old clothes.

"It was easier than checking books out of the library," Stryker said with a smile.

"Yeah, and that was a good thing, because I forgot my library card," Rod chortled. Both young men laughed. Stryker walked over to the desk. He closed the lid on the small notebook computer. He unplugged the telephone cord and plugged it back in to the telephone that was sitting on top of the desk. Then he picked up the notebook and held it under his arm.

"Let's go." Mr. Bunson waved the children toward the door. "No talking."

Astrid, Emily and Josh headed out into the hall. Rod and Stryker walked in front while Mr. Bunson walked behind the three prisoners. They followed the hallway for about fifty yards, then turned left down a new section of the hall. They walked another twenty yards. Rod opened a door. They walked up another long section of hallway and turned right. The floor sloped gradually upward toward a closed door. They stopped when they reached the door.

"My car is just outside this door," Mr. Bunson said. "I want you three to get into the back seat of my car. Remember, if anyone makes even a peep, I'm going to use this gun, you got it?"

The three prisoners nodded. Rod opened the door. He

looked both ways and then stepped outside into the darkness. Stryker walked outside behind the guard. Astrid, then Emily and then Josh walked through the doorway. They were behind the library in a small parking lot reserved for faculty members. There were several parked cars, but no one was into sight.

"Into the car," Mr. Bunson hissed. He reached into his pocket and pulled out his car keys. He gave them to Stryker. The boy with the beard set the notebook computer on the roof of the car. Then he unlocked the trunk. As Rod laid the laundry bag inside the trunk, Stryker unlocked the car doors.

"Now inside." Mr. Bunson waved the gun slightly. Emily started to get into the car.

Suddenly, all around, lights flashed on from the tops of the buildings. The whole parking lot lit up.

"Police! Police!" a voice roared over a bullhorn as officers sprang out from behind parked cars and a big air conditioner. Three police officers rushed out behind them from the hallway they had just been in.

Mr. Bunson looked frantically around and then dropped the gun to the pavement. He held up his hands. Rod tried to run through the parked cars, but two policemen easily tackled him. In a moment he was wearing handcuffs. Stryker just looked around in confusion as the police surrounded him. Three police cars pulled into the parking lot, their sirens blaring and lights flashing.

Emily felt someone cutting the heavy tape off her hands. As the tape came off, she heard a familiar voice.

"Emily! Josh!" Her father ran from behind the corner of the library. Both children ran to their father's outstretched arms. Soon they were all squeezed together in a three-way hug. Astrid smiled as she watched the reunion.

Mrs. Hathaway cut through the crowds of police and campus security personnel. She walked over to Astrid and gave her a big hug. Dr. Morgan looked over at the girl with blond hair.

"Thank you for saving my children, Astrid," Dr. Morgan said.

Astrid smiled and then looked at her feet with embarrassment. Mrs. Hathaway gave Astrid another big hug. By the time she let go, Emily was waiting. Emily handed the girl with wild blond hair the tan notebook computer.

"I think this is yours," Emily said. Astrid smiled as she took the computer into her hands, her many silver earrings twinkling from the flashing red and blue lights of the police cars.

# Chapter Eleven

---

# A Book to Read

A few minutes later, the parking lot was much quieter. The flashing lights of the police cars were turned off. Mr. Bunson, Rod Williams and Danny Stryker were each sitting in the back of a police car.

The police had given Astrid a blue cold-pack to put over the bruise under her eye. Mrs. Hathaway had brought out cans of soda pop to Astrid, Emily and Josh. They sipped from their cans and watched the police work.

Mr. Clark, the museum director, had already arrived. He shook his head in amazement as the police removed the two heavy volumes of the Gutenberg Bible from the laundry bag. Accompanied by several policemen, the guards carried the volumes back into the tunnel to return them to the museum.

"How did you do it?" Emily asked.

"It was really pretty easy," Astrid said. "The university system for e-mail has a quick-note system. I've got my computer configured so I can get a note ready to send with two keystrokes. I can close the note with one keystroke so no one can see it on the screen. Stryker wasn't always watching exactly what I was doing, so when I got a chance, I started typing a note to Mrs. Hathaway. I knew they were probably going to use the tunnels to escape, but I didn't know where until you two arrived. Stryker really stopped paying attention when you all showed up, so I was able to finish the note and send it to Mrs. Hathaway's computer."

"I was never so surprised in all my life to see Astrid's note pop up on my computer screen," the librarian said. "I called campus security immediately, and they called the city police."

"I didn't know what to think," Astrid said. "I guess I was praying that Mrs. Hathaway was sitting where she'd see her computer."

"Well, you see, you are learning how to pray." Emily smiled at her new friend. "God answered your prayer."

"Yeah, I guess he did," Astrid replied.

"I didn't know university students bought and sold tests," Josh said.

"Unfortunately, cheating is more common than you would think," Mrs. Hathaway said. "Cheating and stealing and lying, it's all bad business, but big business. But when the police get Stryker to tell who bought those tests, we'll be able to stop some of the cheaters."

"We'll go after every lead we get," said one of the policemen who was standing near Mrs. Hathaway. Then he turned to Astrid. "We should get you to come down to the station and help us with our computers. We run into problems every other day. But you can't live without them these days. Those guys would have gotten clean away if they had known this young lady knew."

"That's right," Dr. Morgan said. "I still can't believe they actually stole the Gutenberg Bible. Astrid, I knew you were a whiz with computers, but I didn't know how much. I may need to give you extra credit in class. Of course, you already have an A anyway, so I don't think it would make much difference."

"I'm sorry about breaking in to your system, Dr. Morgan," Astrid said softly.

"Don't worry," Professor Morgan replied. "Emily told me all about it. Of course, what you did was wrong, but under the circumstances, I think your parole officer will understand. I'm certainly not going to complain or press charges. I am going to do one thing, though."

"What's that?" Emily asked.

"I'm going to make my password more difficult to guess," Dr. Morgan said with a smile.

"Oh, Daddy-o," Emily said. "I like your password just the way it is."

"They're getting ready to take away those thieves," Josh said triumphantly.

"They're going?" Emily asked. "Wait! Wait!"

"What for?" her father asked.

Emily ran over to the nearest police car. Mr. Bunson was sitting in the back seat staring straight ahead. Handcuffs were locked around his wrists. The policeman sitting in the car looked out his opened window.

"What can I do for you, Emily?" the officer asked.

"Well, he wanted to get a Bible tonight," Emily said. "There's no reason he should go away empty-handed."

Emily pulled her small New Testament out of her pocket. She gave it to the officer.

"I can't think of a more appropriate going-away gift," the officer said with a smile. "Where he's going he'll have plenty of time to read it and think about it too."

"I know I'm going to be reading my copy more," Astrid said with a grin.

"Well, I think Mr. Gutenberg would be very happy to hear that his Bibles are still inspiring people to read," Professor Morgan said with a smile. Emily laughed and gave Astrid a big hug. They were still hugging as the police car drove away.

Don't miss the next book
in the Home School Detectives
series!


Here's a preview of
John Bibee's
*The Mystery of
the Vanishing Cave.*

# Chapter One

---

# The Hole
# in the
# Ground

Nothing out of the ordinary would have happened that day if Rebecca hadn't spotted the unusual hole in the ground. The three girls were in a hurry to get back to camp from their morning hike. Rebecca Renner, Julie Brown and Emily Morgan were all in Cabin Nine, and they felt that Cabin Nine had a reputation to uphold.

All ten cabins were in a race to get back to Camp Friendly Waters. Since the girls had come over the big hill instead of going around it like the other campers, they were sure they would reach camp first, grab the red flag and gain ten points for good ol' Cabin Nine.

"Hurry up!" Emily said to the others as they walked up the steep, rocky side of the hill. They finally left the trail and entered the large, flat, open area at the top of the hill. The clearing, about the size of two football fields, was covered with short rough grass. At the upper end of the clearing, huge piles of rocks and boulders climbed up into the sky. At the very top of the hill sat a distinctive giant boulder called Moaning Rock. Jutting out against the clear blue sky, the big boulder looked majestic and awesome. The big boulder had a hole all the way through it which made a moaning noise if the wind was blowing from the southwest, or so the local people said. None of the girls had ever heard so much as a peep from the giant boulder, however.

"This is a great view up here," Emily said as they stopped to catch their breath. "You can see for miles. It's too bad the highway is so close."

To the north, in the valley below, the four-lane road snaked through the countryside. Near the highway, bulldozers and dump trucks moved along a dusty dirt road.

"It looks like they're building a new road into the camp." Julie took a swig out of her water bottle.

Emily nodded. "They're the ones making the big blasting noises with dynamite to clear out the big rocks. That's what Mr. Sam says."

"I heard one of those ka-booms the first day we got here," Julie said. "It sounded like a bomb going off and made the ground in camp shake. I wonder if earthquakes feel like that."

"Hey, look at this hole," Rebecca called to the others. She was on her hand and knees where the clearing stopped and the pile of rocks and boulders began.

"Come on, Rebecca!" Emily yelled. "If we don't keep moving, we won't get the red flag. You want to beat Shelly and all those girls in Cabin Six, don't you?"

"They're dying to beat us," Julie said. "Especially after Rebecca teased her about that snake in the creek."

"Shelly almost fell into the water, she was so scared," Emily added. "But she did find that broken arrowhead. She was really bragging about it. We need to hurry, Rebecca, or we'll lose."

Rebecca didn't answer. She bent over the hole trying to see inside.

"What's down there?" Julie asked as she ran over.

"I don't know." Rebecca leaned farther over the hole to peek. The hole angled down steeply into the ground.

"I don't see any animal tracks."

"Me either," Rebecca said eagerly. "You'd see tracks for sure if animals lived inside here because the dirt is so soft. The dirt looks fresh, as if it was just dug."

"Do you think someone was digging?" Emily said.

"I don't see any footprints or piles of dirt like someone's been digging with a shovel." Rebecca leaned farther down into the hole. Her brown eyes shone with curiosity. "I wonder what's down there?"

"I do too," Julie said.

"Come on, Shelly and Bernice will beat us back to camp," Emily said. But Rebecca wasn't paying attention. She searched the ground quickly. She ran over to a rock about the size of a volleyball and tried to pick it up, but it was too heavy.

"Let me help you." Julie ran over to her friend.

"Let's take it to the hole," Rebecca grunted as they lifted the rock. Taking tiny, awkward steps they carried the big stone to the hole.

"Let go on three," Rebecca said. "One, two, three . . ."

The two girls dropped the rock into the hole. The round stone hit the soft dirt and then rolled down into the darkness. The ground seemed to rumble for a moment, and then the sound disappeared.

"That's a deep hole," Emily said finally. "I thought I heard an echo or something."

"Me too," Rebecca said.

"You better watch out," Emily said. "You might scare a skunk out of there. Like the song goes, 'I stuck my head in a little skunk's hole, and the little skunk said, "O bless my soul, take it out, take it out, remove iiiiiiitttttttttt." ' "

The three girls laughed. That was one of the songs they sang around the campfire. Singing silly songs was one of the best parts of being at camp.

They had already been at camp for seven days and would be there another full week. Camp Friendly Waters was owned by a Cherokee family who were Christians. The two-week sessions were divided up for girls only or boys only.

Rebecca loved Camp Friendly Waters. It was her first time to visit. She and Emily and Julie were the only girls to come from Springdale that session, but other kids in their church had been there before. The three girls from Springdale all stayed together in Cabin Nine, but there were seven more girls in Cabin Nine from different towns and states.

Rebecca loved the outdoors and all the activities of camp. They could swim and hike and even go horseback riding. She especially liked all the sports and games they played. She was a fast runner. Her favorite sport was soccer, but she liked playing softball, basketball and volleyball too. She was sort of short for basketball, since she was only ten and one of the younger campers. But her quick speed and good ball-handling skills made up for her lack of size.

The day hikes were also lots of fun. Going up and down the winding trails between trees and rocks made Rebecca feel like an Indian scout. Mr. Littledove, the owner of the land, was supposed to give a talk at one of the upcoming campfires about the history of the Cherokees. Rebecca was really interested in learning more Native American history.

Like Emily and Julie, Rebecca was home schooled. All the girls had studied several units through the years on Native American history and culture. She had heard that Mr. Littledove would also show the campers his collection of arrowheads and other artifacts. Rebecca had a keen interest in old tools, weapons or decorations of historical value. She had been hoping all week to find an arrowhead, but so far she hadn't had any luck. Like the other girls, she was envious when Shelly from Cabin Six had found a broken arrowhead that afternoon by the creek.

Rebecca could be very determined and almost stubborn at times. She forgot about everything as she stared down curiously at the hole. She even forgot about beating Shelly and the girls in Cabin Six who acted snooty whenever their cabin won a contest.

"I really don't think it's an animal hole," Rebecca said to the others.

"Who cares what kind of hole it is?" Emily said. "Shelly and her gang will beat us back to camp if we don't get moving soon."

"We still have some time to investigate." Julie got a drink from her water bottle, shrugged off her backpack and dropped it on the ground where the other girls' packs soon landed.

Rebecca got on her hands and knees again and peered down into the hole. She saw small flecks of white stone. She picked up one of the tiny broken pieces.

"This is flint," Rebecca announced as she turned it over in her hands.

"So what?" Emily said.

"Most arrowheads are made of flint because it's hard and can be chipped away easily to make sharp edges," Rebecca replied. "This is Cherokee land. I bet there could be lots of arrowheads around if you knew where to look."

"Like this?" Julie dug into the dirt and smiled as she pulled a white triangle-shaped piece of stone from the edge of the hole.

"It *is* an arrowhead!" Emily said. "Wow! You really found one."

Rebecca's eyes widened at the discovery. She ran away from the hole and picked up a long wooden stick. When she returned, she began using the end of the stick to loosen the dirt around the edge of the hole.

"Maybe there's more," Rebecca said eagerly as she dug faster around the edge of the big hole. The loose dirt fell away in chunks and rolled down into the hole. The other girls found sticks and began digging at the edge of the hole too.

"There's lots of pieces of flint." Julie dug at the ground by her feet. As dirt kept rolling into the hole (which was about a foot across), the area around the hole got wider and wider.

"Stop!" Rebecca yelled. She bent over and picked up a grayish piece of stone. She brushed away some dirt.

"A broken arrowhead," Emily said.

"It sure is." Rebecca smiled. "And look. Even though it's broken, it's bigger than the one Shelly found. I beat her! Wait till she sees this one. She'll turn green with envy. Of course, yours is the best one of all, Julie."

"I'm the only one who hasn't found anything." Emily

made a pretend face like she would cry.

The other girls laughed and said, "Then let's keep digging."

The girls stood around the edge of the hole and began to pound at the dirt. The dirt edge kept crumbling away and falling into the hole until they had dug a wider and wider area around the hole—first three feet, then four feet. But the size of the original, inner hole stayed the same. All three pairs of eyes were trained on bits and pieces of rock in the falling dirt.

"Wait!" Emily shouted. She bent over and snatched up a piece of rock. She turned it over in her hand and frowned.

"It's flint, but it's not an arrowhead," she said sadly.

"Let's stay at it." Rebecca picked up her stick and pounded it down. For a few minutes the dirt flew again. The pit around the hole steadily grew until it was almost six feet across. There were lots of chips and pieces of flint lying on the dirt.

"I think we should stop, you guys," Julie said.

"It's a great hole, isn't it?" Rebecca said with a smile.

"But look how big this pit around the hole is getting," Julie replied and pointed down. "Dirt keeps going down the hole, but it's not filling in. I'd think it would start to fill up by now."

"Then it must be a deep hole." Rebecca shrugged.

"That's what I mean," Julie replied. She bent over and poked her stick down into the darkness of the hole. She waved the stick around against the dirt walls. "I can't feel the end of it. It sort of curves down under Rebecca's side and gets bigger. It almost seems like a tunnel or something."

"It's just a hole," Rebecca said. "Let's look a few more minutes for arrowheads."

"I want to find one since you all found one." Emily began digging again. "I'll be the only one without an arrowhead."

"I think we should stop." Julie stared down into the pit around the hole. "The ground beneath my feet vibrates when you pound your stick."

"What do you mean?" Emily asked.

"Come stand by me," Julie said.

The two girls walked around the edge of the hole to their friend. They stood side by side, six tennis shoes pressed against one another in a line.

"See if you feel anything when I pound my stick." Julie raised the stick and then slammed it down at the edge of the hole with a thud.

"Did you feel that?" Julie asked.

"The ground sort of vibrates," Rebecca agreed. She pounded her stick down in front of her feet. The stick dug into the ground, prying a huge hunk of dirt away from the edge. The chunk of dirt burst apart as it fell into the pit. Some of the bigger hunks of dirt rolled down into the black hole at the end of the pit. Rebecca hit the ground again.

"Did you feel it?" Julie asked.

"Yeah, it shakes beneath your feet." Emily hit the ground with her stick. "You can feel it even more over here." Emily struck the ground again a few more times in different places.

"Look! We're making a crack!" Rebecca pointed at the ground behind her. A small chasm had appeared in the dry ground. Rebecca turned and jabbed her stick down into the chasm. "Wow!" The crack in the ground quickly widened to almost three inches across and four feet long. "Did you see that?"

"It looks like an earthquake hit it," Julie said. "Too bad our brothers aren't here. They'd love helping us."

Emily hit the ground, and the crack grew even longer. The

little chasm snaked away from the pit in a jagged uneven path and then circled around back toward the hole at the far end. Rebecca walked over to the end of the growing chasm and pounded her stick down into it. Before she could pull her stick back up, the ground suddenly shifted and then dropped.

The three girls screamed as they lost their balance. Emily bumped forward into Julie, who was knocked sideways into Rebecca, who was closest to the edge of the pit. Rebecca put her hands out to catch herself and realized she was dangerously close to the dark hole.

The other two barely kept themselves from falling, but Rebecca hit the soft dirt inside the pit with her outstretched arms. The dirt cushioned her fall, but she still tumbled forward as her hands slid downward. The small girl flipped and landed on her back. She felt dizzy as she looked up into the wide open sky from inside the pit.

As she struggled to sit up, she grabbed at the giant dirt clod that held Julie and Emily. As she pushed down on the dirt to raise herself up, the big chunk of dirt began to move again. It slid suddenly down into the pit toward the hole. The three girls screamed again as they all fell this time. Arms and legs jerked and thrashed as the big shelf of dirt kept sliding.

Rebecca braced her foot at the edge of the mouth of the dark hole. The big clod of dirt shoved into her back but then stopped moving.

"That was too close," Rebecca said breathlessly. "I'm afraid to move my legs."

"Don't worry." Julie struggled to sit up. "We'll help you." As Julie started to stand, the ground seemed to groan beneath them. The dirt walls of the pit shook, and little bits and pieces of rock and dirt fell down. The ground shifted and then moved again. The floor of the pit near the edge of the hole broke away.

Rebecca fell downward into the darkness. She didn't even have time to yell. The other two girls rolled forward and somersaulted down into the hole behind Rebecca. A jumble of arms and legs and flying hair disappeared down into the darkness as the ground swallowed them up completely.

*Also by John Bibee*

THE SPIRIT FLYER SERIES

During the course of a year, the ordinary town of Centerville
becomes the setting for some extraordinary events.
When several children discover that Spirit Flyer bicycles
possess strange and wondrous powers, they are thrust
into a conflict with Goliath Industries—with the
fate of the town in the balance.

**Book 1**  *The Magic Bicycle*
**Book 2**  *The Toy Campaign*
**Book 3**  *The Only Game in Town*
**Book 4**  *Bicycle Hills*
**Book 5**  *The Last Christmas*
**Book 6**  *The Runaway Parents*
**Book 7**  *The Perfect Star*
**Book 8**  *The Journey of Wishes*

*Available from your local bookstore or*

InterVarsity Press
Downers Grove, Illinois 60515